a taboo t

REnNER'S
Rules

Mandy,
Be a good girl !
♡KWebster

K WEBSTER

I'm a bad girl.

I was sent away.

New house. New rules. New school.

Change was supposed to be…good.

Until I met him.

No one warned me Principal Renner would be so hot.

I'd expected some old, graying man in a brown suit.

Not this.

Not well over six feet of lean muscle and piercing green eyes.

Not a rugged-faced, ax-wielding lumberjack of a man.

He's grouchy and rude and likes to boss me around.

I find myself getting in trouble just so he'll punish me.

Especially with his favorite metal ruler.

Being bad never felt so good.

Dedication

To the naughty man who taught this girl everything
she knows.
I love you, Mr. Webster.

"To love is nothing.
To be loved is something.
But to love and be loved, that's everything."
—T. Tolis

K Webster's Taboo World

Welcome to my taboo world! These stories began as an effort to satisfy the taboo cravings in my reader group. The two stories in the duet, *Bad Bad Bad*, were written off the cuff and on the fly for my group. Since everyone seemed to love the stories so much, I expanded the characters and the world. I've been adding new stories ever since. Each book stands alone from the others and doesn't need to be read in any particular order. I hope you enjoy the naughty characters in this town! These are quick reads sure to satisfy your craving for instalove, smokin' hot sex, and happily ever afters!

Bad Bad Bad
Easton
Crybaby
Lawn Boys
Ex-Rated Attraction
Malfeasance
Mr. Blakely
Renner's Rules

Several more titles to be released soon!

Thanks for reading!
K

a taboo treat

RENNER'S
Rules

Prologue

Adam

Summer of 2002

Pop! Pop! Pop! Pop! Pop!

I roar and sling my M14 around, my finger pulling the trigger to hit the bastards who've snuck up on me.

"Bonilla!" I yell, as I spray 5.56 bullets at several Taliban motherfuckers.

He responds by firing from somewhere ahead of me and mows down some more men who are chasing after me like goddamn flesh-eating zombies. I haul ass toward my best friend and the rest of our unit when fire explodes in the back of my thigh.

Fuck.

I've been hit.

Another burning punch to the back of my right shoulder and I go down hard, face first. The flesh rips from my cheek as I slide across the hard dirt.

I'm going to die.

Right here.

At nineteen fucking years old.

"Renner!"

The popping of the gunfire all around me becomes muted and fades. I'm dying. It's happening. Fuck. I'm not ready, dammit.

"Renner!"

"Renner."

Sounds of war have disappeared altogether and the only thing that can be heard is the hum and beeping of the machines beside my hospital bed. The pain medicine has long since worn off and I shudder at the realization, my hand blindly reaching for the button to call for a nurse to bring more.

"Renner."

It takes me a moment to fully blink away my daze and when I do, I discover my best friend Mateo Bonilla staring down at me. His black brows are pulled together in concern.

"Hey," I grunt, my voice a choked hiss. Scanning the table beside me, I seek out the ice water that will help my parched throat. I remember where I'm at. Same place I've been for the past two weeks.

Hell.

Not really, but it sure feels like it when the nurses wheel me down to physical therapy each day. A bullet completely shattered my left kneecap, entering in from behind. It ricocheted, destroying ligaments and bone, but what nearly ended my life was when it nicked my posterior tibial artery. And had I not had a medic just feet from me when I went down, I would've bled out before anyone realized what had happened.

Luckily, I had Mateo.

He dragged me to safety and applied a tourniquet.

My best friend saved my life.

"How are you feeling?" he asks, his gaze raking over my face.

I know I look like shit. Road rash ripped away part of my left cheek, forehead, and chin—it's a miracle my eyelids remained unscathed. The nurses have done a great job of distracting me every time I mention it. I haven't had the balls to look in the mirror yet.

"Been better," I grunt, then grit my teeth when a throbbing wave of pain ripples up my leg. "Can you get a fucking nurse in here?"

Mateo finds a nurse and twenty minutes later, I'm flying high, happy as hell. Usually, he leaves once

I get pulled under, but today he lingers. I hang on to clarity enough to finally get the words out without breaking down. The last thing a man wants to do is bawl like a fucking baby to his friend.

"Te," I murmur his nickname. "Thank you."

He chuckles and shakes his head. "It was nothing."

I pin him with a hard glare. "It was everything. You're the reason I'm still here, man. I owe you big time."

"Yeah, yeah," he says, a smile tugging at his lips. "When you get better, I'll call in a babysitting favor. I get no booty from the old lady when we have a two-year-old squatting in our bed."

I smile, but I don't have the energy to laugh. He talks nonstop about his kid. One day I'll meet her and let him and his Puerto Rican goddess of a wife go make more babies.

"I can babysit the kid for a night," I tell him, "but you only need what? Three minutes?"

"Fuck off, gimp," he jokes.

I flip him off and we both grow quiet. Despite our jokes, we were both shaken up pretty badly after that day over in Afghanistan. Half our unit didn't make it. Mateo puts on a brave face, but I know he's mentally dealing with the same shit I am. It's going to be a long road ahead of us.

"I leave for Tampa next week." His eyes flicker my way, pain reflected in them.

"For how long? Taking the wife and kid on a vacation?"

He scrubs at his jaw. "I got stationed there."

My gut hollows out. Mateo and I've known each other for a year, ever since I joined the Marines at eighteen. Not seeing and working with him every day comes as a shock.

Not that I can work anymore anyway.

"Don't do that," he grumbles. "I've seen too many of our guys dig themselves into a hole of self-pity and despair. They never climb back out. You need to get better and get the fuck out of here, man. Go home. Back to Momma."

I shoot him the bird again. "As soon as I get out of here, I'll be right there with you."

"No," he says with a sigh. "Not with those injuries. You're done, Adam. Get better and finish college. Make something of yourself that doesn't require you to carry a gun. Relax and enjoy life. Find yourself a wife."

Before 9/11, I'd planned to get my degree in secondary education. I wanted to teach and perhaps get into the administrative side, like my mom. She was vice-principal at Brown High School, where I went to school, for twenty-three years. But then those motherfucking terrorists tried to destroy America and I had a change of heart. Teaching seemed unimportant when I could be out there making a difference—killing assholes who tried to kill us and those we loved.

"We'll keep in touch," he assures me. "I'll be up for Christmas."

I grit my teeth and nod. "Don't be a stranger. And, Te?"

"Yeah?"

"I still owe you that favor."

He flashes me a wide grin. "Don't worry, gimp, I'll call that shit in one day."

And with that, I watch my best friend walk away.

CHAPTER One

Adam

Present

"I didn't do it." Zane Mullins sits sprawled out across from me, a smirk tugging at his lips. I know the fucker did it because the camera footage says so.

"Destroying school property is grounds for expulsion," I say with a heavy sigh.

He runs his fingers through his messy black hair and shrugs. "I don't like going to school anyway. Hawkins is an asshole."

"Don't curse," I grumble. He's right, though. Jake Hawkins is an asshole. But he's this school's basketball coach and valued by most people in this town. "Destroying school property when you're eighteen

1

years old means we could have you arrested."

This gets his attention.

He sits up, no longer in a slouched position, and frowns. "Dude, don't be like that."

I straighten my tie before standing. "You can't write derogatory statements on Coach Hawkins' office door. Bottom line. Or on anyone's door for that matter."

"So it's just like that? You're going to call Sheriff McMahon and have me taken to jail?" he demands, his tone increasing with anger.

I scrub at my unshaven jaw and glance out the window. We've been back from the Christmas break three days and Zane is already on my radar. This kid stays in my office and for some reason, I keep giving him chances.

"Zane, you can't keep doing this without punishment."

"Whatever, man," he grumbles.

For a brief moment, his hard features soften. He's the kid who three years ago led the basketball team to a championship, despite being a freshman. His next season, though, he broke his leg and his basketball career went down the toilet. Gone was the smiling, athletic kid. Now we have this bitter prick who lives to terrorize everyone, especially Hawkins.

"What do you propose I do?"

At this, he rolls his eyes. "You're the principal. Do what you want."

My phone buzzes in my pocket, but I ignore it as I mull over what I want to do. He needs guidance. The kid is spinning and spinning. I need to stop this.

"Sit tight," I instruct as I stride from my office.

Leah Compton, my secretary, brightens when I stick my head out the door. "Can I help you, sir?" She pushes her chest out a bit, but I ignore her. Leah's been flirting with me for five years, ever since she came to work at Brown High School. I never return her advances because she's fucking married, for crying out loud.

"Can you get Kerry to come see me? Tell her to bring Zane Mullins' file."

At the mention of our new guidance counselor, Kerry Bowden, her smile falls. "Of course."

Ever since Kerry got hired on, Leah acts as though she's a threat to whatever it is she thinks is going to happen between her and me. Truth is, neither one of them is a threat. I don't date married chicks, and I'm not into dating my staff either. Tough shit for both women.

While we wait, I take a seat, ignoring the always burning pain in my thigh and behind my knee.

Taking those bullets was one of the scariest days of my life. Not a day goes by where I don't remember.

"How'd you get those scars?" Zane asks, his voice unusually soft.

I glance up to see him staring at the left side of my face. They're mostly not noticeable. One might think they were acne scars or something at first glance. Each day, I carry another reminder of that fateful day. When my face was shredded by dirt and rocks. The flesh is mottled and uneven, but the pink has long since faded. I can grow a beard on my cheeks if I want and years ago I did to hide. Now I don't give a fuck anymore.

"Afghanistan," I say.

His brows lift in surprise. "Ouch."

I give him a forced smile. The door to my office opens and Kerry steps in. Today she's wearing a fitted pencil skirt and flowing white blouse that accentuates her full tits. Her blond hair has been twisted into a tight bun and her black-rimmed glasses help her achieve a hot librarian look. She's pretty, I'll give her that, and had I met her in a bar or something, I would've asked her out. But she works for me and I don't fucking go there.

"Good afternoon, Principal Renner," she greets, her cheeks blossoming pink for a moment before she

4

regards Zane. "Mr. Mullins."

He stares at her tits long enough that she pulls the file up to block his view.

"Have a seat," I instruct and motion to the chair next to our school's biggest troublemaker.

She sits on the edge of the seat and flashes a polite smile Zane's way. "What can I help you with?"

"How are his grades?"

"All right," Zane answers.

I lift a brow in question as Kerry flips through the files. "Mostly Bs and a couple of Cs."

Color me surprised. "Can the Cs be brought up to Bs?"

"Considering they're in PE and algebra, I think so."

"I fucking hate PE," he grumbles, earning a gasp from Kerry.

My leg burns and I sympathize with him. Injuries are no joke. They sometimes follow you for decades or even your lifetime. I can see how it might be hard on a kid like Zane.

"Change his elective," I tell her. "I want him out of PE. Make him an administrative assistant here in the office. He can help Leah, you, and myself." I glance up at him. "Stop cursing or I'll make you write an essay on the evolution of curse words in different cultures and eras."

"Fine, man," he huffs.

Her lips purse together like she might argue with my instructions, but she decides to bite her tongue. "Is that all?"

"What's the deal with algebra?" I ask him.

He shrugs. "It's stupid easy."

"Stupid easy?" I challenge. "If it were stupid easy, you wouldn't be making a C."

"I don't care anymore. I told Ms. Hogg I already knew all of the work, but she didn't believe me. So now I don't care." He shrugs his shoulders again as if this solves the problem.

"Pull him from Hogg and put him in Long's class," I instruct.

This time, she argues. "Coach Long teaches AP pre-calculus. If he's doing poorly there, how will he keep up in that class?"

I rub at the tension on the back of my neck before pinning them each with a stern glare. "Long will keep him in line and I'll have him keep me updated on his progress. I want Zane meeting with you every Monday after school to go over his grades and his plans for college."

"I'm not going," Zane tells me.

"Yes," I grunt, "you are."

He glowers at me. "This is stupid."

"This is my requirement if you want to keep from getting arrested," I bark out, making Kerry jump.

"Whatever," he concedes.

"Every Monday?" she questions, suppressing a look of distaste.

"And then I want you to see about getting Coach Long to train with him."

"I can't run track!" Zane's outburst has him heaving, his face burning red.

I lean across my desk. "Then you'll walk the track."

"Unbelievable," he mutters.

"When I got hit over in Afghanistan, I wasn't sure I'd walk again. You have to keep your body moving. With Coach Long, I'll see to it that you're with him a little a few days a week so he can work with you one on one. You won't have a whole class full of people watching you."

His anger melts away and he gives me a clipped nod. "Fine. Anything else, Warden?"

I chuckle. "Nope. Now get out of my office and don't cause any more trouble. I really don't want to have to call your dad."

The three of us all tense slightly. Zane Mullins'

father, Felix, is a district attorney who's running for the state senate seat. I went to high school with him and hated his guts back then. Age has only made him more of an asshole. He thinks he owns this town and everyone in it because he has money. A pain in the fucking rear.

"Tell Hawkins to stop riding my ass," he snaps.

I let his curse word go. "Hawkins won't be your problem anymore. Coach Long will be." I smirk at him. Despite Everett Long being tougher and broodier, he's actually a great teacher and coach. He'd be a good role model for Zane. Hawkins is a whiney bastard who cheats on his wife any chance he gets. I don't have much respect for Hawkins.

"Miss Bowden, keep me posted on his progress. I want him graduating on the honor roll. And I definitely want his future plans laid out in concrete by the end of the school year." I tip my head and give her another stern look that says this is not up for negotiation.

She smiles and excuses herself.

"Am I free to go?" Zane asks.

"You're free but stay out of trouble."

He flashes me a wide grin. "I can't promise that at all, Principal Renner."

I chuckle as he leaves. My phone starts buzzing

8

again, so I quickly retrieve it to see who's on my ass knowing full well today is a school day. When I see my friend Mateo's name, I frown. We were close back in the day, but once I moved back home, we drifted apart. He's not on Facebook and old-school as hell. The only catching up we get to do is the occasional text. I know he's been busy with the freight company he's a partner and investor on in Florida, but honestly, I haven't kept up much more than that.

"Hey, man," I greet when I answer the phone.

"Renner," he says, his gravelly voice reverberating through the line. "How's life treating you?"

"Same as last time," I say with a chuckle. "Still the principal at Brown. How's the wife and the little girl?"

The line grows quiet for a moment before he speaks. "Valencia died this past summer."

I blink rapidly in confusion. When we were overseas, he showed me pictures all the time of his very healthy, very beautiful, very voluptuous wife. "She what?"

"Breast cancer," he says, a bitterness in his tone. "We had plenty of time to say our goodbyes, but it's been hard on our baby girl."

I think back to the pictures of his daughter. Dark hair and wide brown eyes like her mother. Fuck, this is shitty and sad. "I'm so sorry. You should have told me. I would've come to the funeral, man."

He brushes me off. "It's fine. Valencia was loved and we had a private burial in Puerto Rico. It's not what I'm calling about."

"I'm sorry," I mutter again, at a loss of what to say.

"I need a favor."

"Anything."

"Don't agree so fast because it's a big one," he says.

"Te, you saved my life. I'd do anything for you. No matter how much time has passed since we've last seen each other or talked. It doesn't matter. Name it and I'll help. I owe you."

"Fuck," he grumbles. "It's my daughter. She's in trouble."

I stand from my desk and start pacing my office. "Is she sick? Hurt?"

"No, nothing like that." He sighs. "She's been getting into trouble a lot at school. Running with a bad crowd this year. Her grief is changing her personality. I don't know what to do anymore. I'm fucking helpless."

Kids. That's something I do know.

"Does she need someone to talk to?" I ask.

"More than that." Another heavy sigh. "I caught her with some drugs and boys in her room. I just know she's off having sex and shit. I'm afraid some idiot is going to knock her up. All the memories are too hard on her. If she could just get away for a few months and start over, I think I could get my little girl back."

"Sex?" I hiss. "She's what? Like fourteen? I'm so sorry, Te."

He chuckles. "No, man. You were always a dick at keeping up with shit. She just turned eighteen over a few months ago. It's one of the reasons why I worry. Had she gotten picked up somewhere with those drugs on her, she would've gone to jail. My girl would have a record." He curses under his breath. "I feel like an asshole for asking this, but…"

"Yeah?"

"Can she come up there? You could keep an eye on her and make sure she stays in school. Maybe a change of scenery would be good for her. We're making some changes at the company—a lot of traveling on my part—and I've been inundated with work when she needs me most. Being a principal and all, I thought maybe you could help her."

The very idea of having to babysit a teenager has my skin crawling, but she's not just any teenager.

She's Mateo's. And I owe him everything.

"Of course, man," I say without hesitation. "My house isn't fancy like yours, though. She'll have to get used to roughing it."

"Still living the lakeside cabin life? I always knew you were a simple motherfucker," he says, amusement in his tone.

I don't tell him the reasons why I have the cabin.

I need the peace.

I crave it.

"Simple house note too," I retort. "Not all of us live in fancy-ass condos with our own valet service."

He laughs. "I like to spend my money."

"I like to keep mine."

"Thanks, Adam. This means the world to me. If you need me to save your life again, just give me a call," he jokes. "But seriously, though, thank you. I don't know how else to help her."

"We'll get her straightened out," I vow. "I promise."

"I knew I could count on you."

CHAPTER Two

Adam

The weatherman predicts snow, but I don't need the television to tell me that. I can smell it in the air. There's a wet, brisk bite to the air, which is why I'm chopping some wood. A couple of years ago, I miscalculated my wood and when I got snowed in, I nearly froze my ass off. I won't be making that mistake again.

But despite it being just below thirty degrees today, I'm hot as hell. My shirt drips with sweat and if I didn't have a teenager on the way, I'd shed it and finish my task. The ax is heavy, but it's perfect and I keep it sharp just for this task. Some birds caw in the distance as they fly over Lake Newell. I'm just wondering what I'll make for dinner when I hear a car crunching gravel in the distance.

Mateo and his daughter.

Unease skitters through me, but I quickly breathe through it. I deal with teenagers all damn day. I can handle one for extended periods. I'll lay down the law and she'll have to obey. Bottom line. For Te, I'll make sure she stays on the straight and narrow.

It's been a few days since he called, but it's given me time to prepare for a house guest. Mom came over and deep cleaned my cabin while sprinkling in her two cents. She cooked meatloaf, so I didn't even mind the lecturing about how inappropriate it would be for a student and her principal to share a cabin. I'm extremely professional in all aspects of my career. And after we recently dealt with our own guidance counselor at the high school going to jail for messing with some students, I've been extra vigilant.

An expensive black sedan comes into view, kicking up dust along the way, before pulling in next to my midnight blue Ford F150. Of course Mateo would have a driver bring him from the airport rather than rent a car like a normal human. Money has made him a bit of a diva.

The car door opens and he steps out. Same guy I remember. A little shorter than me and stockier, but an infectious grin that used to have all the women in the vicinity turning his way. He beams at me before sauntering my way. His black suit is probably more expensive than all of mine combined.

"Renner," he greets, bypassing my outstretched hand and going in for a hug.

I hug my friend. "Bonilla."

We pull apart and he pretends to sniff his suit in disgust. "They make showers, man. Use them."

I chuckle and shrug. "Where's the kid?"

He glances over his shoulder, then frowns at me. "She's not happy."

"I can't say I blame her. Her dad just pulled her out of her school, moved her to a different state, and is dropping her off to spend the remainder of the school year with her principal so she'll stay out of trouble. I think it's safe to say you're her least favorite person right now." I rub at the back of my neck, the ever-present tension making its throbbing presence known. "She's going to be okay. I won't let anything happen to her and I'll protect her as if she were mine."

He lets out a sigh of relief. "Thank you." The wind whips around us and some sleet pelts me in the face.

"Bad weather is rolling in tonight. They say by

tomorrow we'll have snow," I tell him as I peek at the sky.

"Which is why I changed my flight back home from tomorrow to two hours from now. I have a meeting Friday afternoon that I can't miss," he says with a groan.

I keep my features impassive, but it irritates me that he's going to dump his daughter and run. Sure, we're friends and have been for a long time, but he doesn't know if I've changed in the past sixteen years or so. I'd expected him to stay for dinner and give his daughter time to get acclimated.

"Elma!" he hollers. When she doesn't open the door, he curses under his breath before stalking over to the vehicle. He wrenches the door open and gestures at my small cabin with his hand.

Turning to give them some privacy, I swing my ax into the log I was hacking away at and brush my palms off on the front of my jeans. When I look over my shoulder, I'm confused. For a moment, it's as though I'm staring right at his wife, Valencia.

Dark, almost black hair is twisted messily on top of her head. Her face is painted in such a way that her lashes accentuate her wide, deep brown eyes and her lips are stained a pouty red. But what has my attention is her outfit. It's cold as fuck and she's dressing like she's still in Florida. She wears a soft gray open sweater that goes all the way down to her calves. Under the sweater is a tight black V-neck tee that plunges deep, revealing way too much cleavage.

My dick twitches and I grit my teeth.

Quickly skimming over this girl's tits, I'm even more shocked to see her bare belly button and a silver piece of jewelry hanging from it. She wears frayed jean shorts that are ridiculous in this weather. Her boots are the only thing winter-ready and they're those expensive fuzzy boots all the girls at the school wear. Uggs or some shit. But what looks even more goddamn ridiculous are her black knee-high socks.

Just an entire outfit of all the wrong clothes.

Mateo needs to get his head out of his ass.

At my school, she'd get sent to the office wearing this shit.

"Adam, this is Karelma. Last time you saw her she was about a year old," Mateo says, a proud grin on his face.

She's texting and chewing her gum, refusing to look up. It grates on my nerves.

"Nice to meet you," I rumble. "I hope you brought warmer clothes."

At the sound of my voice she lifts her gaze to mine. Her expression changes from bored and irritated to shocked. It's then I realize she's probably looking at my scars or how I'm sweaty as hell. I didn't think out this whole first impression very well.

"Karelma—" I start, but she interrupts me.

"It's Elma." Her smile is fake before she goes back to texting.

"Sweetheart, I have to go. Be a good girl for Adam and I'll call to check on you this weekend." He holds out his arms for a hug.

She peels her gaze away from her phone long enough to step into a side hug from her dad. Mateo doesn't seem bothered by the fact she's being kind of rude. He simply kisses the top of her head.

"We'll be in touch. Take care of my girl," he says as he hands me her suitcase. His phone rings and before he makes it back to the sedan, he's barking out orders to someone. I don't get so much as a wave before he's gone.

"Let's get you inside before you freeze to death," I mutter.

She grumbles something about me killing her in my cabin, but I ignore her. I'm used to teenagers mouthing me when I turn away. I focus on not limping even though my leg hurts like a motherfucker with the cold weather heading in. The last thing I need to do is give her any ammunition against me.

She's quiet as I show her my small cabin.

"I'll sleep out here and you can take my room," I tell her as I motion for the only room in the cabin.

She makes a sound of disgust. "My bedroom back home is bigger than your whole entire house."

Ignoring her comment, I take her suitcase to my room and set it on my bed. She stands in the doorway with her lip curled up and her nostrils flaring.

"I can't fucking believe he sent me here," she hisses under her breath.

I want to get onto her for her language, but I bite my tongue this time. "Make yourself at home. There's some leftover meatloaf in the fridge for dinner. Just heat it up in the microwave. I'm going to take a shower and then we'll talk about your class schedule for tomorrow."

"Yippee," she mocks. Her tongue darts out and licks her juicy red lip, causing my dick to jump again.

Fucking hell.

CHAPTER
Three

Elma

his can't be happening.

This can't be happening.

I stare at Principal Renner from the kitchen when he emerges from his bedroom freshly showered. Somehow, he becomes impossibly hotter. Dad never mentioned Adam was so gorgeous. I'd expected some old, graying man in a brown suit. Not this.

Not well over six feet of lean muscle and piercing green eyes.

Not a rugged-faced, ax-wielding lumberjack of a man.

His wet brown hair has been combed back, but a piece falls over his brow, giving him a boyish look despite being just as old as my dad. The gray Brown

High School T-shirt he's wearing molds against his sculpted body. Principal Renner definitely works out. His jeans are old and worn but somehow look stylish on him. He's barefoot and my gaze falls to his masculine feet.

Who knew feet could be sexy?

"Did you find dinner?" His voice is deep and throaty. It rumbles its way deep inside of me. I'm embarrassed that his voice freaking turns me on.

"I don't like meatloaf." I lift my chin in the air. "Sorry, dude."

His jaw clenches and a flash of fire flickers in his eyes. It makes me want to do it again—to see how the greens in his eyes seem to flame with darker hues. "Call me Adam around the house. It's Principal Renner at school, though."

I roll my eyes and text my best friend Rita.

Me: *This fucking bites.*

Rita: *I still can't believe you left me. This is so unfair. Who's going to party with me?*

And by party, she means me watching her crazy ass so she doesn't get taken advantage of. More than once she's gotten high and nearly lost her mind. It's one reason why I never did any drugs. Someone had to take care of Rita.

Me: *Jason? Last weekend you had no issues*

ditching me to make out with that asshole.

Rita: He's totally an asshole. I should have stayed with you. I miss you.

"Elma," Adam barks, making me jump. "Put the phone away."

I arch an eyebrow at him. "Excuse me?"

"It's not the time, nor the place."

"Okay, *Dad*," I mock. All thoughts of him being hot are squashed as irritation flits through me. I start to reply to her when my phone gets pulled from my grip. "Hey!"

He slides my phone into the pocket of his jeans and I narrow my eyes at him. If he doesn't think I'll go after it, he's crazy. But then he crosses his muscled arms over his sculpted chest and gives me a look that says: try it.

"Give it back," I order.

"Not until you show some respect. We're two strangers and I'm tasked with taking care of you. The least you can do is talk to me like a normal human."

"Do you talk to all your students like this?" I snap.

"Only the little shits."

I gape at him. "I'll tell my dad."

He arches an eyebrow in challenge. It sucks he's so hot because he's a total douchebag.

"He'll come right back."

Something resembling pity softens his features. "He's not coming back. At least not any time soon."

My gut hollows out and I peel my gaze from his. Tears sting at my eyes, but I quickly blink them away. He's right and I know it. Dad's always so focused on work. I love him, but once Mom died, he became obsessed with the company he part owns. I've practically raised myself since her death.

"Whatever," I grumble. "I won't eat."

He grunts as he makes his way over to the fridge. I pout with my arms crossed over my chest, ignoring the shiver that runs through me. I was warned it was cold here, but it's not like I had anything better to pack clothes wise. I'll be damned, though, if I ask this guy for something warmer to wear. I'm still lost in my thoughts, staring out the window as snowflakes blow around, when I get a whiff of something savory and delicious. My stomach growls.

"Eat," he instructs as he sets down a plate on the table.

I turn to see a slice of meatloaf, some mashed potatoes, and green beans steaming from the plate. My stomach whines again. With an eye roll meant to piss him off, I throw myself down into the chair and try not to look so desperate to eat a home cooked meal. Now that Mom's gone, I usually fend for myself since Dad always works so late. Cereal. Mac and cheese. Pizza. Mom used to cook the best dinners. Just thinking about her and her nightly meals where she'd flit about the kitchen as though it came natural to her has me once again fighting tears.

This sucks.

Leaving Florida.

Coming to this cold hell.

Staying with the freaking principal of the high school I'll be attending.

It just sucks.

"My mom makes the best meatloaf," he tells me as he settles across from me with a piping hot plate of his own. He pushes a can of Coke my way before diving in.

I pick up the fork that's on my plate and stab at the meatloaf. One bite later and I'm in heaven. Apparently, I do like meatloaf. The food settles my attitude and I wolf it down greedily. When I finish, I find him staring at me with a brow arched.

"Hungry?"

Heat floods my cheeks and I'm suddenly self-conscious. "Are you saying I'm fat?"

His eyes widen. "What? No. How the hell would you come to that conclusion?" Sincerity flickers in his green eyes and I relax slightly. I've got some curves—more than most girls I know—and it makes me constantly worry that people are judging me for it. I'm happy with my breasts and usually my ass. That is, until I'm hunting for jeans and none of them seem to fit my round rear.

"Can I have my phone back?" I ask, changing the subject.

He leans back in his chair and assesses me. I want to squirm under his intense stare.

"Later. For now, I want to talk."

I let out a huff. "Okay, so talk."

"What do you do for fun?"

The laugh that escapes me is mocking. "What do I do for fun? Oh my God."

He glares at me. "I'm being serious."

"I play on my phone," I deadpan. "So, as you can see, I'm bored." I smirk at him and revel in the way the vein in his throat pulsates.

"What else do you do? Sports? Band?"

"Band?" I shriek and scrunch my nose. "Ew. No."

"Don't be such a princess. Band is hard work."

Another eye roll. "Okay, Principal Renner."

A muscle in his neck ticks and if he wasn't so annoying, I'd have the urge to lick it. But he's annoying and rude. I definitely don't want to lick it.

Well, maybe just once to see what he tastes like.

"You're going to find something to do with your time while you're here. Something constructive. Something useful for your future."

Holy shit, he's worse than Dad. He's like a double dose of Dad. Ugh. My life is over. I retract my neck licking thoughts effective immediately.

"No. Hell to the no." I lift my chin and hope I'm putting up my best glare of intimidation.

He rises from his seat and I try not to focus on the way his bicep bulges when he leans across the table to pick up my plate. With his head lowered closer to mine, I get a whiff of his manly scent that has me thinking even stupider thoughts than simply licking his neck.

"You will. My house, my rules." He flashes me a panty-melting grin that has me flushing all over. "My school, my rules."

He starts loading the dishwasher and whistling. Cheerful asshole. There's no way in hell I'll be joining any extracurricular activities. Five months and I'm out of here. I'll go back to Florida with my friends and…

And what?

I'll figure it out when I get there.

CHAPTER Four

Adam

Really, Mateo?

I can't believe he entrusted me with his bratty teenage daughter.

Fuck my life.

Reluctantly, I handed her phone back after dinner and she's been glued to it ever since. It's a shame she's not nicer. I spend a lot of time out here in the middle of nowhere at my cabin. Alone. For a second there, I actually looked forward to having someone sharing my space, dinners, and conversations. When I'd seen her, I even allowed the basest male part of me to admire how goddamn beautiful she is and appreciate the fact I'd get to look at her all the damn time.

But then she opened her mouth.

Stuck her nose in the air and acted like one of the brats at school.

A harsh reminder, but one I clearly needed so I wouldn't lust over my friend's hottie daughter. As though my eyes have a mind of their own, they stray from the news on the television over to her bare legs from her knees to her thighs. Smooth, golden light brown skin. She's kicked off her shoes and has her legs tucked under her as her fingers fly over her phone. I'm sure she's talking all kinds of shit about me to her friends.

"It's cold," she says with a pout without looking up.

"You're not in Florida anymore, Dorothy."

She darts her dark brown eyes my way long enough to give me a condescending look I'm used to from my students before she lets out an obnoxious sigh and starts texting again. I stifle a frustrated groan and rise from my recliner. I find a worn quilt from a closet and toss it at her.

"It's getting late. Do you want to shower now or in the morning before school?" I ask as I watch her situate herself under the blanket.

"Tomorrow."

She smiles at her phone and it lights up her features. I'd like to see her do that more often. Not that fake shit she's dazzled me with tonight.

I reach for the remote and turn off the television. While she texts, I rummage through my messenger bag and retrieve the schedule I printed up for her once I had her transfer papers from her other school. I set the paper on the coffee table and cross my arms over my chest.

"Your schedule," I say, a bite of irritation in my voice.

When she continues to ignore me, I yank the phone from her grip and pocket it once again.

"Hey!" she yells, her nostrils flaring in fury as she glares up at me. "What's your problem?"

"Right now? You. You're rude as hell. I'm having a hard time coming to terms with the fact my friend raised such a brat," I snap, completely out of character for me. Normally, I'm cool when the kids try to rile me up.

But with her?

She pisses me off.

"Who do you think I learned it from?" she bites back. The venom is missing, though, and for a moment she looks as though she might cry.

My anger is immediately snuffed out. I sit on the coffee table and hand the paper to her. "I just want you to be prepared tomorrow. It's a big school and

31

you're starting in the middle of the year."

She swallows and gives me a curt nod before taking the paper. "I hate math."

"You're good at math," I challenge. "Straight As until this past semester. You dropped to a C by the end of the term. But typically you're an excellent student in math."

"Stalker much?" She doesn't look up at me and bites on her lip as she studies the schedule. "What's the last class?"

"Office admin assistant. Basically you'll help the secretary, the guidance counselor, and myself. Run notes to students and teachers. File stuff. Things like that."

"Boring," she grumbles.

"It was that or band." I arch a playful brow at her.

Her lips quirk up on one side and she regards me with a half-friendly smile. "This will do just fine. But AP pre-calculus? Really?"

"When I spoke to your guidance counselor at your old school, she assured me you were more than capable. You'll do fine. Just try not to fall in love with Coach Long. It's a problem." I stifle a chuckle because Coach Long is a bear and it bothers him that half the student body and teachers follow him around like lost puppies.

"Don't worry. I'm not into old geezers." She purses her lips and holds out her palm. "Can I have my phone back now?"

I pull it from my pocket and relinquish it once more. "I'm lenient here at the house, but you can't have your phone in class. Make sure it stays put away." My tone is gruff because I can't stop staring at her mouth. The more she tugs on her bottom lip with her teeth or wets it with her pink tongue, the more inappropriate my thoughts get. "I'm going to grab some stuff from my room and then you can head that way."

Not waiting for an answer, I stride from my living room into my bedroom. I shut the door behind me and run my fingers through my hair. My dick is at half-mast and irritation flits through me. I'll have to call up one of my buddies and see if they want to hit the bar or something so I can get my dick wet. I've gone far too long without a piece of ass and if I go much longer, I'll be whacking off to images of an ass I can't have. My cock twitches in my pants and I groan. Just the thought of her ass has heat burning through me.

She's Mateo's little girl.

As if doused in cold water, my dick softens.

I cannot allow myself to even go there. Thoughts

are dangerous because thoughts become actions. From here on out, I'll be strictly professional. I have to be.

$\sim$

The pain.

Oh God, the pain.

They're coming for me. I can hear their voices. The popping of their weapons. Holy shit, I'm going to die. This fucking sucks.

Explosions and gunfire thunder in my head.

Pain assaults me from every nerve ending.

I curl up in the dirt and attempt to protect my organs.

Someone grabs me and starts dragging, but I scream and flail.

"I've got you."

"I've got you."

I wake up in a cold sweat in the dark. I'm disoriented and not sure where I'm at. The bullets are no longer whizzing past me. I'm no longer running for my life.

A shudder ripples through me and I let out a hiss of terror when a hand grabs mine.

"Shhh," she murmurs. "I've got you."

I blink in the darkness and it takes me a moment to realize I'm at home in my living room. The soothing voice that belongs to the hand clutching mine is her.

"Elma," I croak.

I relax against the pillows but don't let go of her hand. The horror is still attacking my nervous system. Selfishly, I hold onto her comforting grip for a moment longer.

"You had a nightmare." Her voice is soft and soothing as she runs her thumb along the back of my hand. "Everything is fine."

I stiffen when her other hand rests against my chest that's soaked my shirt with sweat. I'm sure she can feel the way my heart is thundering beneath her fingertips. Neither of us says anything. When my anxiety lessens and I'm not on the edge any longer, she stands and releases my hand. The comforting aura I was just blanketed in gets ripped off of me and I reach for her.

My palm curls around her thigh. Her bare thigh. She lets out a shocked gasp and my cock lurches to life. Blood rushes through me, chasing away the chilling fright that haunts me more often than not.

Take your hand off her.

A groan escapes me and I utter out my words.

"Thank you."

I let her go.

And fuck if it doesn't take everything in me not to grab her again.

She walks away from me and soon the bedroom door closes with a soft click. My cock is hard and aching in my sweatpants. I need to come so I'll relax and go the fuck to sleep. I'm too wound up and having a drop dead, gorgeous temptation in my house doesn't help at all.

I slide my palm beneath the band of my sweats and close it around my throbbing dick. It's hot and hard as hell in my grip. I try to think up images of the new guidance counselor, because at least she's nearer to my age. Blond hair. Big tits. Plump lips.

I yank at my cock brutally, forcing myself to think of Kerry.

But then, like the sun parting through clouds, I see her.

Elma.

My mind roams to the way she sprawled out on the couch earlier with her bare thighs on display. I'd briefly imagined what her flesh would look like there if I sucked her skin. Purple and bruised, no doubt.

I groan at the thought of parting her sweet thighs and inhaling what's between them.

"Fuck," I hiss.

So close.

Don't be a pervert, man.

Kerry.

Blonde. Big tits.

Nope.

I see brown eyes and nearly black hair in my fantasy. Slender fingers touching herself over her shorts. The image is too much and I explode. Cum jets out, hot and furious, soaking the bottom of my shirt. I lie there a moment, my chest rising and falling in rapid succession as I try to sort out what the fuck just happened.

I am a pervert.

I just jerked off to thoughts of a damn teenager. A student. Someone I'm in charge of taking care of.

Angrily, I yank off my soiled shirt and use it to clean up my mess. Once I'm relaxed again, I try to formulate a plan.

And with her, I'm going to need a big-ass plan.

Professional.

I need to be professional.

I'm the goddamn adult here after all.

Using techniques my therapist taught me for my panic attacks, I breathe in deeply and exhale slowly. I focus on my calm place. The lake. The birds. The wind whistling through the trees.

I close my eyes and drift off.

Splashing right there in the middle of my happy place in a red bikini is her. A sacred place in the back of my mind has now been contaminated. And stupid fucking me does nothing but stare.

I'm so screwed.

CHAPTER *Five*

Elma

"Elma!"

I groan against the pillow that smells of him. Masculine and woodsy. Delicious. "Go away."

The door creaks open and light blinds me.

"Up. Now. We'll be late."

With a huff, I sit up in bed and glare at my intruder. As soon as I catch sight of him, all anger slips away. This morning, he's dressed in a light gray suit. His shirt is crisp and white. A black, thin tie hangs from the perfect knot at his throat.

"Elma," he barks again, his hands going to his hips as he glares down at me.

When I lift my gaze, I admire how handsome he looks today. His chocolate brown hair has been styled in a sleek, fashionable way. The scruff from yesterday is gone, giving me a perfect view of his severe, sharp jawline. His full lips are pressed into a line as he stares at me impatiently.

"I don't feel good," I lie.

His eyebrow arches up and he smirks at me. Dear God, this man looks good no matter what expression he's making. "I don't care."

The flames kindling inside of me are snuffed out at his attitude. "You're an asshole."

He clenches his jaw and his green eyes harden into a shiny jade color. "You have exactly fifteen minutes to get ready and get in my truck."

"Or what?" I challenge.

A wolfish grin tugs at his lips. "Or I drag you out of here in your pajamas. You can start your first day in what you're wearing."

Ugh. Prick.

I slide past him out of the bed and revel in the choked sound he makes behind me. I'm wearing a T-shirt and a pair of pink panties. I seriously doubt he'll let me go to school looking like this. When I peek over my shoulder, he's staring at my ass with his mouth slightly parted. It gives me satisfaction to know I have the principal stunned speechless.

Without another word, he turns on his heel and

storms from the room. The door slams shut behind him, making me jump. My smile slowly fades away as nerves set in.

A new school.

Oh, God.

Tears prickle at my eyes, but I blink them away as I hunt for clothes. I don't want to go to school in this dumb town. Starting over in your senior year is the worst. After more like twenty minutes, I'm dressed and made up. I've checked my phone several times looking to see if Dad was checking on me, but I come up empty. My heart aches, but it isn't surprising. Since Mom died, Dad has slowly been pulling away from me. I don't think he realizes it, but he has been.

A hard knock on the door startles me.

"What?" I snap.

"Are you dressed?"

"Yep."

The door flies open and Adam glares at me. His nostrils flare as his gaze skims over my outfit. "Nope. Try again, little girl."

I gape at him. "Excuse me?"

"You're not wearing that."

I look down at my outfit and huff. I'm insulted. My outfit is cute. "Why the hell not?"

41

He scrubs at his face with his palm before pinning me with an incredulous stare. "Because it's snowing, sweetheart."

Heat burns my cheeks, but I don't tell him I don't have anything warmer. Instead, I lift my chin and spit out my words. "I'll live."

"Actually," he says in a cool tone, "you won't. Your ass will be freezing before we even make it to the truck. You can't wear that in the middle of winter."

I pull my long sweater around me and regard him with a lifted brow. "Look. I'm warm. Problem solved."

He flicks out his wrist and checks his watch before gritting his teeth. "Let's go."

As we walk out of the cabin, I can't help but wonder what happened to the man who cried out in his sleep as nightmares plagued him. The fear in his voice was bone-chilling. It had me running from his room and into the living room in an effort to calm him. We didn't speak. Just held hands. He'd eventually calmed and I was free to go.

Until he grabbed my thigh.

My neck heats from the memory. I'd gone back to the room, crawled under the covers, and attempted to bring myself to orgasm after that. I was frustrated and unsuccessful, but not from lack of trying. I wanted to march right back in there and demand he take care of what I couldn't complete.

Instead, I fell asleep emptier than before.

All alone in a cabin with my principal.

It's laughable.

As soon as the front door opens, I let out a shriek. Icy air slides in and finds its way through the thin fabric of my sweater. I shiver and try not to slip on the icy porch. I'm thankful to see the truck is already running. It's snowing slightly, flakes fluttering around us. Adam is on a mission as he stalks to the passenger side and wrenches the door open. My heart stutters in my chest for a moment at his gentlemanly action. None of the guys I dated before ever opened my doors.

My cheeks blaze crimson. I'm not dating Adam. He's charged with taking care of me in my father's absence. When I reach the open door, I stare up at the tall truck in confusion.

How am I supposed to get up there?

As if reading my thoughts, two strong hands grab my waist. Then, as though it's as effortless as lifting a sack of feathers, I'm hoisted into the truck. I'm so shocked at how he gracefully put me in his truck that I can't even form any words of gratitude.

He slams the door shut and is soon safely inside with me. I steal a glance at him as he backs the truck up. He's all man as he maneuvers the truck back between two massive trees and then forward again. His giant frame fills his side of the truck, whereas I'm dwarfed in the passenger seat.

"Meet me in my office after school and we'll head home." His head turns and he quickly looks me over. "Can you refrain from telling anyone about our arrangement for the time being?"

I smile. Oooh, this is good. Principal Renner wants me to be his little secret. The thought is dirty and I clutch onto it desperately. "Sure."

He relaxes and flashes me another one of his panty melting grins. "I think everything's going to be just fine."

∽

"You did what?" Adam's voice is cold and deadly as he shoots daggers at me with his eyes.

I've been at this hell hole of a school for all of two hours and I'm already sitting in the principal's office. "He was being an ass." That's my only defense for how I acted in Coach Long's class. Adam was right. Coach Long is freaking gorgeous. "All I said when he yelled, and he did yell for the record, when one of the kids wasn't paying attention was—"

"I heard," he snapped. "'I bet if you took off your shirt, you'd have everyone's attention. Especially mine.'" His jaw clenches and his green eyes burn with fury.

I start giggling. A nervous habit. Plus, it's kind of funny that I've managed to already piss off so many people and I've been here half a day. "I was just trying to help."

He drags his attention to the window where it's heavily snowing now. His arms are crossed over his chest. He's long lost his jacket and his sleeves have been rolled up, revealing too much yumminess for a high school principal. Muscular, tanned forearms. Sexy veins that protrude and just beg to be licked. Colorful tattoos that I'm dying to run my fingertips over.

"You have a smart mouth," he grumbles, his broad shoulders tense.

"My mouth is good for a lot of things," I mutter, my tone thick with insinuation. "But mostly I use it for being smart."

He snaps his head my way and his hot glare rakes over me. "Get back to class. I don't want to see you back in here for the rest of the day."

"Or what?" I challenge.

He growls. He actually growls. My core clench-es in response and suddenly I'm slightly dizzy in his presence.

"Or I'll call Daddy."

I laugh, the sound harsh. "Okay. Get right on that."

"Your dad should have whipped your ass a lot more when you were a kid," he mumbles under his breath.

I gape at him in shock.

"Go, Elma," he bites out. "Now."

Zane.

The hilarious friend I made today is hot but to-tally not my type. Plus, he's practically drooling and in love with someone else. It's funny to watch the way he catalogs her every move.

"You should take a picture. It'll last longer," I taunt.

He swivels in his desk chair and flips me the bird. The secretary, Leah, lets out a bitchy huff that has Zane and me snorting with laughter.

"I have plenty of pictures," he whispers and

waves his phone. He mimics jerking himself off and I die laughing.

"Miss Bonilla!"

The sharp, prickly voice has me jolting in my seat. Miss Bowden frowns at me as she drags her disproving gaze down the front of my chest.

"What?"

"That is unacceptable clothing," she hisses, her cheeks blossoming bright red. "Leah," she admonishes. "Why didn't you say anything?"

"Oh," the secretary murmurs. "I was busy working on some things for Mr. Renner." The tightness in her tone reveals she doesn't like Miss Bowden any more than I do.

Miss Bowden points past me. "Go see Mr. Renner. Right. Now." She punctuates each word in a furious manner. I don't miss the way she darts her gaze over at Zane briefly as to see if he's checking me out.

He's too busy stifling his laughter. I flip him off this time.

"Now," she screeches.

I slide off the desk and brush against Zane's shoulder.

"Good luck," he mutters as I walk by.

Ignoring the evil glare coming from Miss

Bowden, I march out from behind the front desk and over to Adam's door. It's ajar and I can hear him typing away on the computer. With my chin lifted, I push through it and close the door behind me.

"Yes?" he says without looking up.

"Miss Bowden said you wanted to see me," I say in the most innocent voice I can muster.

At the sound of my voice, his attention snaps my way. Our eyes meet for a heated second before his roam lazily down my front. As soon as he takes in my attire, his brows furl together angrily.

"Elma!"

"What?"

The off-the-shoulder T-shirt I'd been wearing earlier has long-since been shed, along with my sweater as well. I stuff my hands into the pockets of my cute army-green cargo skirt and shrug. It's just a tank top. It's not my fault my boobs are big.

"That…" He waves at my outfit as though it's personally offended him. "You can't wear that."

"How come?"

His eyes dart to mine and his jade-colored orbs blaze. Heat. Lust. Desire. I don't miss the way he stares at me as though he wants to help me with my clothing problem by getting rid of it altogether. I shiver at the thought.

Almost imperceptibly so, his gaze softens. He rises from his chair and snags his blazer from the back of it. "Wear this."

I stare at his offering as though it's riddled with fleas. There's no way I'm wearing the principal's jacket.

"No."

"Elma." His voice quakes with warning.

When I refuse his jacket, he storms over to me. He hangs it over my shoulders. Like I'm a child, he grips my wrists and forces them into the sleeves. He's not satisfied until he has it buttoned and my breasts are no longer on display.

"There," he says, his voice gruff.

But when his eyes drift down to my thighs, he lets out a frustrated breath.

"Actually. No. Take it off."

I start laughing at him. "What? Why?"

"That skirt…" His eyes bore into mine. "It's too short."

"It's fine."

"It is *not* fine." He rakes his fingers through his hair, messing up the styled perfection. "Four inches. Your skirt can't be any shorter than four inches above the knee." He pins me with a furious glare.

"I'm short. You're being ridiculous."

He drops his stare to my mouth and he shakes his head as though to clear his mind. "I'll get Miss Bowden in here to measure—"

"Adam," I whine. "Please don't. She hates me."

His hot eyes flicker and I realize I've said his first name. Backtracking, I bite my lip and bat my lashes at him innocently.

"Principal Renner. If you absolutely must prove this to yourself, then by all means, measure my skirt. Just don't let that woman do it."

He rubs at the back of his neck and darts a nervous look toward the door. "It's against policy for a male staff member to—"

"It can be our little secret."

"You're so damn naughty," he snarls under his breath.

I laugh again and enjoy the way he seems to have completely lost his mind. Driving Principal Renner crazy is fun. He asked and now I have an answer. Him. He's my new hobby.

He rummages through his drawer and produces a ruler. For a split second, a fantasy plays out in my mind where he bends me over his desk and spanks me with the metal ruler. My cheeks flush at that thought, and his jacket that smells too manly and delicious suffocates me with its heat.

"Come here," he instructs, his voice harsh and authoritative.

A thrill shoots down my spine and I obey him. Once I'm standing so close that our chests are nearly touching, I look up at him. His gaze has softened as he greedily drinks up my features. Like a creeper, I inhale him. His scent is even more heavenly straight from the source.

"You're going to make my life hell, aren't you?" He doesn't seem angry, just resigned to the idea.

"I've done nothing wrong."

He arches a brow and the corner of his lips twitch as though he's fighting a smile. "I'll be the judge of that." He kneels down in front of me and my breath is sucked straight from my chest when his strong hand curls around my thigh.

Just like last night.

It feels as familiar and right as it did then.

A strangled sound escapes me as he presses the ruler against my flesh. His hot breath tickles my thighs and I find myself growing wet for him.

"Okay." His voice is gruff.

"Okay?"

"It's fine." His thumb brushes along my skin before he releases me and rises to his full height. "I'd like you to wear the jacket or put your clothes back on. Please, Elma."

I'm flushed and lightheaded after his intimate touch. His husky words seem to vibrate straight to my core. "Yes, sir."

A muscle in his neck ticks and his brows furl together. "So polite."

"I can behave sometimes."

His grin, wolfish and hot as hell, knocks me off my game. I simply stare at how beautiful he is. "If you behaved *all* the time, I'd be out of a job."

CHAPTER Six

Adam

My nerves are on edge. Last night, I was gruff and pretended to bury myself in work on my laptop to avoid her. I can't believe I touched her thigh yesterday in my office. I fucking flirted with her.

So wrong.

And now...now I'm going to be stuck in this house with her.

Alone.

I glare out the window at the shiny layer of ice that now coats everything. Trees, the ground, my truck. The wind howls, promising more icy terror. Mocking me. Reminding me I've fucked up and my punishment is to be trapped inside my house with a tempting vixen. I've already made the appropriate calls canceling school today. Normally, I'd enjoy the day off and lounge around the house watching ESPN and shit.

Today?

I don't know what I'm going to do.

Her alarm starts buzzing from my room and it makes me aware that I've been standing here for an hour glaring out the window contemplating my situation. When she doesn't turn it off, I let out a frustrated growl and walk into my bedroom. She's buried under my covers and if I were a lesser man, I'd crawl under there with her. My cock twitches at that idea and I let out a groan.

She stirs and I start to retreat.

"I'm up," she grumbles as she slaps at her phone.

"Go back to sleep," I bark out, a little harshly. "School's been called. Everything is blanketed in snow and ice."

She sits up in bed. "There's more snow? Like enough to build a snowman?"

Before I can answer, she flies from the bed and runs past me. Her scent swirls around me and my cock is wide fucking awake now. The fact I'm wearing sweatpants does nothing to hide my arousal. She lets out a loud shriek that has my lust-filled thoughts quickly switching to ones of alarm.

"What's wrong?" I bellow as I follow her into the living room.

I find her staring out the window with her palms on the glass. Her dark hair is down and slightly tangled. She's once again wearing nothing more than a tank top and some frilly looking panties. Her tanned legs are for my visual tasting. But it's her round, juicy ass that looks downright delectable.

"Can we build a snowman?" she asks as she bounces on her toes. Her ass jiggles, making my cock painfully hard.

"No," I snap. "It's twenty-three degrees out there."

Her head turns and she regards me with a pout of her plump lips that does nothing to help the state of my cock. "Please, Adam."

I position myself behind the sofa so she doesn't see how my body is responding to her. "No."

Her shoulders slump and she walks away from the window. If I'm not mistaken, her bottom lip wobbles as though she might cry. Guilt surges through me. She makes her way back into my room and climbs back in bed. I can't help but follow after her. Leaning against the doorframe, I watch her lie back on the pillows and begin texting.

Dammit.

I'm really not good at this shit.

Running my fingers through my hair, I leave her be to go make breakfast. Hopefully bacon and eggs will draw her out of her pouty mood. But breakfast comes and goes. And when I ask her to come eat, she says she's not hungry.

The wind doesn't let up and the snow continues to fall. It looks cold as hell out there. Which it makes no sense as to why I'm giving in.

"Elma," I bark from the doorway.

She arches a brow but doesn't look up from her phone.

"Fine."

"Fine what?" Her nostrils flare, but she doesn't look up at me.

"Fine. We'll go build a damn snowman."

Her squeal of delight catches me off guard. But what really throws me off is when she launches herself from bed and flies into my arms. On instinct, I hug her to me and inhale her hair. I'm shocked still for a moment, but then my body heats as I realize how perfect our bodies meld together.

"This is the best day of my life," she murmurs, her breath tickling my neck.

My cock hardens against her stomach and I'm flooded with embarrassment. "Good," I choke out.

"Be ready in ten minutes and we'll go play. I saved you a plate of food. We're not going anywhere until you eat, though."

She pulls away, her cheeks blossoming red, and bites on her bottom lip. "Yes, sir."

Fuck, she's driving me mental.

I give her a clipped nod before bolting from the room before I do something stupid like kiss her sweet mouth. My dick aches to do other things, but I can't go anywhere with her. Just being alone with her in this house is damaging to my psyche. While she dresses, I rummage around in a duffle bag I'd filled with my clothes until I find what I need. Quickly, I dress in the bathroom, then wait in the living room for her. When she emerges from the bathroom, I growl.

"No."

"What?" she asks, her lip curling up slightly.

I wave at whatever the fuck she's wearing and shake my head. "Absolutelyfuckingnot."

"What's wrong with this?" She huffs and puts her hands on her hips, accentuating the curves there. "I'm covered."

"First of all," I grumble, "you're *not* covered. I can see your bra through your sweater." And fuck if her tits don't beg to be sucked on. "And those tights?"

I shake my head in horror. "You'll freeze your ass off. Literally. But secondly, where the hell is your coat?"

At my question, her haughty expression falls and her eyes well with tears. The pretty browns look more like melted chocolate now. Why does she have to be so beautiful?

Softening my tone, I say her name, "Elma."

A tear streaks down her cheek and she drops her arms to her sides. Once again, I feel like a prick. Her father has all but abandoned her here and I'm being an asshole. I step over to her and bring my finger beneath her chin. When I tilt her head up, her black eyebrows are crushed together and her bottom lip pokes out. She's the cutest fucking thing I've ever seen.

"I'm sorry," I tell her and I mean it. "I'm not good at all this. It's just really cold out there and I worry."

Her lips quirk and she gives me a shy smile. "I think that's the nicest thing you've ever said to me."

I laugh and love the way her eyes light up. "Don't get used to it," I tease, my thumb running along her jaw. All it would take would be for me to lean in and kiss her supple lips. One tiny kiss and I'd be so far down the rabbit hole, I'd never climb back out.

My palm slides to the outside of her neck because the urge to touch her is winning out over my sane thoughts. "Where's your coat?"

She frowns and breaks eye contact. "I don't have one. We don't really need them in Florida."

A growl rumbles through me. I really am an asshole. Breaking from her intoxicating presence, I storm over to a closet. I rummage around and find my warmest coat. When I offer it to her, she beams.

"Thank you."

I stare at her for another beat before scrubbing at my jaw with my palm. "You ready to go freeze our asses off, snow girl?"

$\sim$

Holy shit, it's cold.

Playing outside when it's cold as fuck is not my idea of a fun time but seeing her bright smiles, her rosy-colored nose and cheeks, and hearing her adorable laughter has me here for the duration. I'm staring at her pitiful snowman when something hard hits me on the side of the head.

"What the—"

Another icy and painful blast hits me in the face.

"Snowball fight!"

I watch her run as fast as her short legs will carry her, her head turning back every so often to see if

I'm following. My heart races and my blood burns as it rushes through my veins. The very idea of chasing her sets my soul ablaze.

"You better run faster than that, sweetheart," I bellow. "I'm going to get you!"

She squeals and it echoes off the trees. The storm is in full force and I'm worried that things will get worse before they get better. All worrying thoughts dissipate, though, when she stops to lob yet another snowball at me.

It hits me hard in the center of my chest.

This girl should be playing softball or some shit.

I limp, thanks to the cold bothering my injury, quickly through the snow and she doesn't get far from me. With a growl, I tackle her into the snow. We both go down hard and I briefly worry I might have hurt her. But then she's giggling and screeching as she tries to get away.

"Let me go," she cries out.

I grab a handful of snow and smash it against her face, reveling in her laughter. She squirms and fights me until she's on her back. I pin her in the snow and hold her wrists so she can't throw any more snowballs at me.

The snow begins falling heavier, blanketing her hair and face. The tiny flakes land on her eyelashes and she blinks them away. With my gloved hand, I release her wrist and then set to dusting away the snow. She lets out a soft, husky sigh that has my dick at attention.

"You caught me." She smiles at me. An angel. Perfection.

"I'm not letting you go."

Her eyes widen at my words and I want to reel them back in. I meant literally, but then I let my mind wonder so many what-ifs that will get me in some serious fucking trouble.

A shudder ripples through her and her teeth begin to chatter.

"We've been out here too long," I say, my voice strained.

She nods but seems reluctant to want to get up. It takes everything in me not to press my lips to hers. Instead, I pull away and help her up. The wind howls and pelts us with more snow and ice. Like the fool that I am, I tug her into my chest and wrap my protective arms around her to shield her from the storm. She's stiff at first but then hugs me back. With her ear pressed against my chest, all is right in my world.

She's a teenager.

Your friend's daughter.

Worse yet, she's your student.

A groan rumbles from me.

"What's wrong?" she asks, her head tilting up.

I'm once again struck by her exotic beauty.

Kiss her.

Fuck, how I want to.

Her lips part and her brown eyes twinkle with anticipation. My hands cup her cheeks of their own accord. Touching her feels right. It shouldn't, but it fucking does. She flutters her eyes closed before letting out a tiny sigh. I lean forward and run my cold nose against hers.

"Adam," she breathes.

A plea.

She wants me to kiss her.

Fuck, how I want to.

"Elma…"

She stands on her toes as if to reach me easier.

One kiss.

Just one little kiss.

It's just us. Two people. A man and a woman. Easy.

But then I begin to wonder what an outsider would see. Would they think I'm taking advantage of her?

Mateo would beat my ass to a bloody pulp.

I can't fucking kiss her because if I do, I won't

stop. I'll take and fucking take until I own every part of her.

"Oh, sweetheart," I mutter before tilting her head down. I kiss her forehead instead.

A tiny sound of irritation escapes her.

"We need to get you inside," I say in defeat.

Crack!

A limb nearby, heavy with ice, careens to the forest floor. It's then I hear more cracking. Fuck. Things are about to get more interesting.

CHAPTER *Seven*

Elma

"**W**hat do we do?" I ask in horror. When it sounded like the forest was breaking all around us, Adam rushed us inside.

Ice.

The ice is breaking the limbs left and right.

And apparently, it's the source of our sudden power outage.

"We ride it out until the power company gets it restored," he grumbles.

I'm soaked from the snow and shivering. Without the blaring heater on, it's drafty in the cabin. No heat. This is the worst.

"Take your clothes off," he demands, his voice husky.

I snap my attention his way as he tosses logs into the fireplace. "W-What?"

"Get out of those wet clothes, Elma. You'll catch pneumonia." His back is turned to me and I'm embarrassed I'd assumed his words meant something else altogether.

I fumble through the fairly dark cabin until I get into the bedroom. My phone is lit up on the bed and I snatch it up. With frozen fingers, I read through the many texts from my old friends. I find one from Zane that has me smiling.

Zane: Where do you live? My dad has ATVs. I could come get you.

Yesterday, I never mentioned to him I'm living with our principal. For some reason, I wanted to keep that information to myself.

Me: Outside of town by the lake. It's too cold anyway.

He replies instantly.

Zane: Wussy.

I stick my tongue out at the phone but then notice my battery life is depleted after Rita's incessant texting. Apparently she's having a boy crisis. Or boys crises. The one she kissed last night saw her kissing someone else between classes earlier this morning. Now, the boy from yesterday called her a slut.

Rita kind of is a slut.

I snort and reply to her.

Me: Sorry, honey.

Rita: Late much? Were you ignoring me?

I roll my eyes. Rita is demanding.

Me: No, we had a snow day here. I was playing outside.

Rita: Ew. No. We're going to the beach later today.

I have a pang of jealousy that I won't get to go swimming with my friend, but then I realize hanging out with Adam isn't the worst.

Me: Have fun, babe. Talk later.

I toss my phone on the bed and worry that if we don't get the power restored soon, I won't have any link to the outside world. I'll be stuck in this cabin with Adam as my only source of entertainment.

Heat surges through me.

Again, not the worst thing to happen to me.

Quickly, I shed my soaked clothes and throw on something warmer. I've just slipped out of the room to find Adam standing in front of the fire with no shirt on. I stare in shock. His back muscles are flexed and decorated in colorful ink. The sweatpants he dons are hanging low on his hips. A shirt is fisted in his grip and the other hand reaches for the blazing flames.

"Hey," I squeak out, my eyes glued to his perfect body.

He turns and I get a glorious view of his chest. More tattoos. Muscles galore. What has me speechless, though, is the way his oblique muscles seem to make a path pointing straight to the bulge in his sweatpants. The same bulge that was hard earlier this morning when it was pressed against me. I bite my bottom lip and meet his gaze.

"That doesn't look very warm," he grunts and runs his fingers through his hair. His bicep flexes and I wonder about what it'd be like to lick it.

"I could say the same." I motion at his bare chest with my palm.

He yanks his shirt on over his head and before I know it, his perfect torso is no longer on display. Stupid me and my stupid words.

"You need pants on." His jaw clenches as he pins me with a hard stare.

"Shorts are fine. I have long socks on," I argue.

He rolls his eyes and saunters over to a bag in the corner. When he bends over to rummage in it, I get a prime view of his hard ass. I stare at it, suppressing a moan. My drooling gets interrupted when he tosses sweatpants at me.

"I'll put them on if I get cold." I flash him a fake

smile before prancing over to the fireplace and warm my hands in front of the flickering flames.

He walks up beside me and mimics my action. Our arms brush against each other. I shiver, but it's not from cold. It's from anticipation. He misunderstands, though, and lets out a frustrated sigh. "Put the pants on."

"I'm fine. You're bossy."

I expect him to argue but instead, he wraps an arm around me and pulls me to his side under the guise of warming me up. I settle against his solid body, inhaling his manly scent.

"How are you holding up?" he asks suddenly.

I stiffen at his question. "I'm good."

"Not…not about being here." His fingers tighten around my hip. "About your mom."

A choked sound escapes me. All it takes is one mention of her and tears are stinging my eyes. My chest physically aches as though the pain is all trapped up inside without any chance of escape. Some days, I just want to cut it out of me. "It hurts."

I'm surprised I uttered those truthful words. Dad has asked a few times, but I always put on a brave face for him because I know he's hurting too. With Adam, it's safe to just let it out.

"I'm sorry, Elma."

A tear slips from my eye and slides down my cheek. I sniffle and shrug. "It's okay."

He pulls me to him for a real hug. Being in his strong, sweet embrace does something to me. I feel a crack. Right down the center of my chest. As though, if I'll let him, he'll have the power to crack me right open and help pull the pain from me. A sob chokes me and he squeezes me tighter. His fingers run through my still wet hair and he kisses the top of my head. It's all so intimate and gentle. Since I've met him, I've seen him go through a myriad of emotions. Mostly, he tries to keep his distance with growls and frowns. But sometimes, he surprises me with bright smiles and glimpses of his vulnerability.

Instead of feeding me words that don't help anyway, he simply holds me. I melt in his arms and pray the moment never ends. It's been forever since I felt secure and cared for. Mom is gone and Dad has mentally checked out. Adam fills a hole that has been empty for some time now.

"Have you ever thought about playing softball?" he asks, his voice gruff but gentle.

"I used to play when I was in middle school but…" My chest aches.

"But what?"

"I started playing volleyball in the ninth grade. It was our thing. Me and Mom. She was like the honorary team mom. Everyone loved her." My words come out as a whisper. Now that I'm talking about her, I don't want to stop. Tears steadily stream down my cheeks and I know I'm soaking his shirt with them.

"She was lovely. The few times I met her, I thought she was an amazing woman. Much too amazing to be with the likes of your daddy," he teases with a chuckle.

I let out a small laugh. "Daddy always said she was too good for him, but he just got lucky. He'd tease that she was the one with the bad luck." My smile falls. "Turns out he was right because she got cancer."

"Oh, sweetheart," he murmurs. "I'm sorry."

I cry softly against his chest. I feel stupid, but the release of all the pent-up pain inside of me is freeing. Rita never wanted to talk about my mom because she said it was depressing. To satisfy her, I didn't talk about how sad I was around her. She, being my best friend, tried to distract me with boys and jokes and trips to the mall.

"I miss her," I say, my voice cracking.

He strokes my hair. "I know you do."

Once I've calmed and all that can be heard is the occasional hiccup from my crying, he speaks again.

"Did you leave volleyball back in Florida?"

My heart clenches. "It didn't feel right without Mom on the sidelines."

His fingers tangle in my hair and he tugs until I'm staring up at his brutally handsome face. With the light flickering on the side of his face, I can see the scars better. The flesh is slightly mottled and shadows dance in the indentions that aren't as noticeable during the day. I can't help but reach up and palm his cheek. He flinches and closes his eyes.

"What happened?"

His eyes reopen and a pained expression is etched on his face. "The past. It tried to kill me. I won." He clenches his jaw and looks away.

My heart stutters and aches. I've just bled out feelings in front of him, but he isn't opening up at all. "I see."

His hand wraps around my wrist and he pulls my hand from his face. "It's a story you don't want to hear. But I owe him." His green eyes blaze into mine. "Everything. I owe him my life."

I blink up at him. "Who? Daddy?"

As if being showered with a bucket of icy water,

he shudders and jerks away from me. "Yeah," he grunts. "You hungry?"

My shoulders slump in defeat. It turns out I'm not the only one guarding their heart. I wonder if I'll ever get to hear that story.

CHAPTER
Eight

Adam

I've fucked up royally.

I can't keep my hands to myself for one. But I've been treating her like she's my girl. She's not my girl, though. She's the daughter of my friend. I need to calm the hell down and keep my distance.

Yet, I can't.

All day, she's been avoiding me. Completely shut down. It wasn't fair. I probed her about losing her mother, but I couldn't even share what had happened to me. I took from her and gave nothing in return.

After dinner, she sat in front of the window and stared out into the darkness. Her melancholy mood is screwing with my head. It makes me want to haul her back into my arms and comfort her.

"You should come sit in front of the fire," I tell

her, my voice gruff.

She shivers and shakes her head. "I'm fine."

Irritated, I stalk over to her. "You're not fine. You're cold."

When she makes no moves to get up, I squat and slide an arm around her. She lets out a surprised squeal when I lift her up. I ignore her protest and squirming. With her in my grip, I sit down in front of the fire. She's stiff in my lap for a moment but then relaxes her back against my chest.

"Do you have to do that?" she whines.

"Do what?"

"Touch my stomach like that." She lets out a huff. "I'm fat."

I laugh at her words. "You're what?"

"Oh my God. Stop. You know exactly what I mean."

My palm is over her stomach through her hoodie. She has soft curves that I'm growing steadily addicted to. The girl's crazy if she thinks they're a problem.

"You don't like this?" I ask, toying with her as I squeeze her through her shirt.

"Ugh," she groans. "It's gross."

I tickle her through her shirt and she screams, her entire body thrashing. Once I stop, she settles and it's then I notice my palm has slipped beneath her hoodie. I run my thumb absently over her skin on her stomach.

"I like it," I murmur.

Her breathing is heavier, but she's not telling me no. I should be telling me no. Instead, I caress her stomach in a reverent way. What she's embarrassed of feels soft and sweet to me. I'd love to get my mouth on her stomach and show her how a real man appreciates everything a woman has to offer.

"You're lying."

"I don't know what rock you've been living under for the past couple of decades, but curves are hot."

As soon as the words are spilled from my lips, I regret them and pretend I never spoke them. If she were just some woman I'd met, I'd tell her all of these things and more. But she's not just some woman. She's my student. I'm charged with taking care of her.

Images of her naked and sprawled out beneath me take over my mind.

I'd love to take care of her all right.

"Elma," I murmur, my chin resting on her shoulder. "You're so goddamn beautiful, you're going to get me in trouble."

"Trouble, how?"

I close my eyes and imagine so many ways I'd love to get into trouble with her. "I could lose my job. What we're doing now would get my ass fired so fast I wouldn't know what hit me."

"We're not doing anything wrong," she breathes.

My thumb runs along the underside of her breast. "We are. So wrong, Elma."

"I like it, though."

"Please don't encourage me," I groan. "I'm fucking everything up right now."

She lets out a heavy sigh but doesn't press me any further.

"I should make you a bed out here in front of the fire so you don't get cold," I tell her, my voice husky.

Her head turns and our faces are inches apart. "Just stay a little longer like this. Please."

The tension in my shoulders relaxes. "A little while longer."

"He's bleeding out!"

"Someone hand me my fucking bag!"

"Mueller's been shot too. In the face. He didn't make it."

"They're still shooting!"

"Someone put that motherfucker down so I can focus!"

"He stopped breathing!"

I wake up screaming and thrashing. The pain is as real as it was that day. Fear of dying hangs heavy in the air, suffocating me.

"Breathe."

The voice is soft. Angelic. Sweet. I seek her out in the darkness. I'm cold as fuck and I wonder if death is coming for me. It isn't until warm thighs straddle my waist and her palms splay out over my chest that I actually settle.

"Adam," she murmurs. "You're safe."

I'm desperate to touch her back and I blindly grab for her. My palms connect with skin. Smooth, silky skin. Her thighs are perfect. I can't help but run my hands up and down along the outside of her legs. She shivers against me.

"Want to tell me what you were dreaming about?" she asks.

My chest aches and I shake my head even though she can't see it in the dark. "N-No," I rasp out.

She lets out a sad sigh and starts to climb off me. Panic slices through me. Her comfort is much needed right now. I can't let her leave me just yet.

"Don't go," I plead.

When she relaxes, I pull her to me. Her tits are barely contained behind her thin T-shirt and her hardened nipples press against my chest. She nuzzles her face against my neck, her hot breath tickling me. My hands slide up her thighs to her hips. With her barely clothed and straddling me, my thoughts quickly flit to dirty ones. Images of her completely naked as her tits bounce while she rides me is my favorite and I let that one roll over and over on repeat in my mind. It isn't until she lets out a mewl that I realize I'm hard as a fucking rock.

"Elma," I groan, my self-control holding on by a thread.

She grinds herself against me, making us both let out a sharp hiss of air.

"We have to stop," I growl. But stupid fucking me doesn't want to stop. My fingers dig into her hips, but I don't move her away from me. She's a fantasy come to life pressed against my aching cock.

"I don't want to stop," she breathes. Her hips work back and forth as she rubs herself against me in a way she must enjoy as well based on her tiny moans.

"We need to." I let out a groan. "Elma."

"This feels good," she whispers, as if the confession surprises her. Hell yeah, it does. I could show her many other ways of pleasuring her, all of which involve my tongue.

"Why do you have to be so goddamn beautiful?" I grit out, my hips slightly bucking. "You're making this impossible to resist you."

"So don't resist." Another moan. "Just see where it takes us."

It'll take me straight to the unemployment agency.

"Oh God," she whimpers. Her body shudders against mine.

Fuck.

Holy shit.

She just came by dry humping me.

My cock seems impressed by that notion because without warning, I come with a snarl. Hot semen spurts out and soaks my boxers. She continues to rub against me, drenching her already wet panties. What a literal fucking mess we are.

"Elma. Fuck. That was—"

"Amazing." Her voice is dreamy and sexy.

"You need to go to your room," I rumble out, shame coating my words. "Now."

She stiffens and sits up. "But—"

"Now, dammit!"

As soon as she jerks away from me, I feel like the

biggest asshole on the planet. I hear soft thuds as she runs off and then my bedroom door slams shut.

Jesus Christ, I'm so stupid.

I have got to nip this shit in the bud or I'm going to do something we'll both regret like fuck her. I'm not one of the teenage boys she sleeps around with back home. I'm her goddamn principal. I have a responsibility here. There will be no casually fucking my student. End of story.

I just wish my dick would get on the same page as my head. My heart, though? An ache forms in my chest knowing she's probably crying in bed this very moment.

My heart is a wildcard.

CHAPTER Nine

Elma

Several days later...

"Stop trying to hack into Mrs. Compton's computer," I grumble at Zane.

He lifts her keyboard and hunts for something. When he finds a password written on a sticky note, he laughs. "Bingo!"

"You're going to get expelled," I warn.

"You're no fun," he grumbles. "What's crawled into your ass lately anyway?"

I lift my gaze from my phone where I've been texting Rita. "Nothing."

He rolls his eyes. "Don't lie, El. I can see through that shit."

A smile tugs at my lips. I've known Zane less

than a week, but we've already grown close. It's nice to have a friend in this lonely town. Especially since Adam avoids me every chance he gets. When we lost power a few days ago, we'd sort of connected. Then, after his nightmare, we had a sexually charged moment where we both got off. But then he blew me off and has acted cold ever since. I actually texted Dad begging for him to come get me, but he gave me a distracted bullshit reply that he'd see me soon and to just try harder.

I've tried hard every day to get Adam to look or talk to me. All I get is a few grunts and mumbled words. He doesn't even look at me anymore.

"It's a guy," Zane says knowingly.

My eyes dart to his. "No."

He smirks. Zane is really fucking hot and if I weren't going crazy over a certain grumpy principal, I'd go out with Zane. But Zane is into someone right now anyway. He stares at her with longing and sadness. I know exactly how he feels—wanting what you can't have.

"Come on," he urges. "Tell Uncle Zane all your woes."

"Uncle Zane?" I snort with laughter. "Ew."

"Like you're not into older guys…" He waggles his eyebrows and then makes an obvious show of glancing over into Adam's office.

"What are you talking about?" I hiss.

He leans forward in Mrs. Compton's chair. She's in a meeting with the guidance counselor and Adam. We've been left to our own devices and are clearly unfit to hold down the fort seeing that Zane is trying to hack into one of their computers. "Don't play coy with me, Elma Louise."

I laugh and flip him the bird. "That's not my middle name."

"And that's not the point," he says with a smug grin that could melt any girl's panties right off. "The point is you're crushing so fucking hard on our principal."

"Even if I was," I huff, "it's not like anything would come of it."

He shrugs as if it's simply a hurdle. "You have to seduce him."

I frown at him. "Maybe I already tried."

His eyes widen. "What?"

"I'm staying with him," I confide. "He's friends with my dad. You can't tell anyone, though."

"No fucking way!"

"Shhh," I hiss.

"So what did you do? Uncle Zane needs all the dirty details for his spank bank."

"Ugh, you're gross," I grumble. "We had a couple of…"

"Fuckfests?" he offers with a wicked smile.

"No!" I shriek. "Moments. We had a couple of moments."

"Lame." He gives me a faux yawn. "Well, unless those moments were naked ones."

"We both came."

This gets his attention because he stands so fast, the chair rolls out behind him and nearly knocks a plant off the back credenza. "You what? Principal Renner and you came? As in you moaned his name and he shot his wad all over the place?"

Heat floods up my neck. "Oh my God. You're so dramatic. Too dramatic for a boy."

"I'm a man," he says with a wink. "And I fucking knew there was something going on between you two. So what's the big problem?"

"He got all weird afterward and has been avoiding me."

He paces around for a moment. "We need a plan."

"A plan?"

"To get him to pull his head out of his ass. I mean, look at you, Elma. You're hot as hell. That old man would be lucky to fuck someone like you."

"Maybe I want to do more than just fuck," I huff.

Like be held. Be adored. Kissed and hugged. Talked to.

"Like anal?"

"Oh my God," I groan. "You're such a freak and hardly a romantic."

He snorts as he takes his seat at Mrs. Compton's desk again. His brows furl together as he taps away on an email. Then, he manipulates some spreadsheets. He has the computer locked again before I can even ask what he's up to. I probably don't want to know, but judging by the dark look behind his normally playful demeanor, I know it wasn't good.

"What did you do?"

"If I told you, I'd have to kill you," he jokes. "Now. Where were we? Oh, yeah, get the principal to fuck you. Hmmm…" He scratches at his jaw as he thinks. "Well, you already dress like a skank, so you've already got step one covered."

"Fuck off," I say with a laugh.

My skirt is short today, but it looks cute with my knee-high socks and combat boots. The sweater I'm wearing falls off the shoulder and shows off my pretty hot pink bra strap. My hair has been pulled into a messy bun and I have dramatic eyeliner wings on today. The coat Adam ordered for me showed up yesterday and while the gesture was nice, it's ugly as sin. It doesn't go with my outfit at all.

"Have you considered trying to make him jealous?" he asks, his brow lifted in question.

My nose scrunches up. "No. How?"

"Come sit in Uncle Zane's lap and I'll show you," he teases.

I laugh and shake my head. "Oh, no. You're always up to no good. I'd end up naked if it were up to you."

His gaze darts out into the hallway before he regards me with a serious expression. "I'm not into you, Elma, so you can trust that I'm not trying to get you into bed. I'm into some chick who's way out of my league. But for you, my friend, I could help make Principal Renner jealous. Are you up for it?"

"Ummm…"

"It's just a kiss."

I laugh because he actually looks innocent saying that. But I know better. Zane is anything but innocent.

"Fine. A kiss but don't try anything freaky. I don't want to have to kick your ass."

He smirks. "Maybe I'm into that sort of thing."

"Whatever. Where are we doing this?"

He pats his lap, his grin wolfish. "Right here."

I roll my eyes but make my way over to him. He grabs my hips and urges me to straddle him. Once I'm sitting on his lap, all too close for comfort, I frown. "Now what?"

"Now we wait until we hear them coming."

"And then?"

"And then I kiss the hell out of you. You better act like you're enjoying it too."

"We're going to get in so much trouble," I whine.

His palms grip my ass through my skirt. "Wouldn't be the first time for either of us. We're both here for a reason. A couple of fucked-up teens whose parents and teachers don't know what to do with them."

"Adam tries," I argue. And he does. Despite him not talking to me, he did connect me with this school's volleyball coach. I'd been angry at first, but all it took was watching one practice before the desire to play was burning through me. Coach Mink said I could try out any time.

"Adam? On a first name basis now?" He lifts a brow.

"You're so annoying."

"You love me," he retorts.

"You're growing on me. Like a fungus."

We both laugh. More laughter echoes ours in

the hallway. I recognize Mrs. Compton's laugh from anywhere. She's always trying to put on a show for Adam. It annoys me when she flirts with him.

"Elma," Zane says, his palm curling around the back of my neck. "Now."

His lips press against mine and I let out a surprised shriek. He gives my neck a small squeeze of support that has me opening my mouth to accept his kiss. I've kissed tons of guys back home. I'm not sure why I'm getting all bent out of shape for kissing Zane. He's a great kisser and tastes good, but he's not the one I want to kiss. His large hand grips my ass, causing me to gasp. I can feel him smile against my mouth.

"Here we go," he says before attacking my lips again with his.

I'm hyperaware that any moment we'll have an audience. The hairs on my arms are standing and I'm stiff in Zane's arms.

"What the hell is going on here?" Adam's voice booms. He's furious and it has me jolting away from Zane. Zane flashes me a conspiratorial smile as I scramble off his lap. When my eyes meet those of Mrs. Compton, Miss Bowden, and our angry principal, I freeze. Both women just seem shocked, but it's Adam who looks positively livid. His nostrils flare and his neck is turning purple with rage.

Oh shit.

"I, uh, I…" I trail off, my eyes prickling with tears. While it was a good idea at the time, now I regret kissing Zane.

"My office, both of you," Adam snaps before storming into his office. The door slams closed and all the pictures on the wall rattle.

I shoot Miss Bowden a helpless stare. She returns a cold glare my way. Her nose turns slightly pink as she regards Zane with a look of disappointment.

"You two are in serious trouble," Mrs. Compton snips as she shoos Zane out of her chair.

I blink back tears as I make my way toward Adam's office. Zane runs to catch up to me.

He ruffles my hair and whispers, "It'll be okay. Trust me."

I swallow and give him a quick nod before following him into Adam's office. He's not sitting at his desk but is instead pacing the floor beside it. When we walk in, he glares at Zane.

"Are you trying to ruin your life by doing stupid things every chance you get?" He seethes, his fury pointed at my friend.

Zane stiffens and clenches his jaw. "Just kissing a pretty girl who deserves to be kissed."

Adam's hands curl into fists. I stare at him, worry niggling at me, and wonder what he'll do. He wouldn't hit Zane, would he? The vein in his neck pulsates, but he doesn't move. I let out a tiny breath of relief.

"This isn't your last school, Elma. You don't get to do…" His intense glare rakes over my outfit, lingering at my tits. "This."

"What?" I chew on my bottom lip and nervously tug at a stray string on my sweater.

"Zane, out. I want you to go to Miss Bowden and tell her I said to find you a fitting punishment. Do as she says. I don't want to see any more of your stunts." He pins Zane with a hard stare. "Understood?"

Zane's brows rise as though he's surprised he isn't getting punished further. He gives me a quick wink that makes Adam growl before exiting the office. As soon as he's gone, Adam walks over to the door and turns the lock.

"You," he murmurs.

"What about me?" I sass with false bravado.

"Kissing him is unacceptable." He challenges me with a heated glare.

"Why?"

"Because I fucking said so," he snaps.

I arch a brow at him. "Because this is school policy?"

He stalks over to me and crowds my personal space. Today he smells spicy and manly. It does crazy things to my hormones. It reminds me of the night he held me and we both got off from dry humping.

"Because I don't like it." He lifts a hand and brushes a strand of dark hair from my face. His features have softened slightly.

"That's a lame reason."

"Nevertheless, it better not happen again."

I scoff at him. "And if it does?"

"It won't."

"How can you be so sure?"

Hard jade-green eyes pierce mine. "Because I'll make sure you remember your punishment every time you even think about kissing him."

"Punishment?"

He grabs my shoulders and twists me so that my back is to him. His palm slides down my back and settles on my ass cheek. "I'm going to whip you like your daddy should have a long time ago."

I choke and let out a startled sound. "You'll what?"

He squeezes my ass and my panties quickly become damp. "Exactly what I said."

"Will it hurt?"

His lips find my neck and he presses a kiss to my

flesh. "I hope so."

A shiver rattles through me. "What if I don't want it?"

He lets out a heavy sigh. "Then you need to tell me right now, Elma. Right fucking now. I am teetering here and you've already given me one push. I'm a grown-ass man. I'm too old to be playing little girl games. If you're just going to tease and not follow through, then you can go accept your punishment from Miss Bowden as well." His lips kiss my throat once more. "But if you're ready to take a dive with me, then you'll accept your punishment from me."

"I…" I'm so stunned by his sudden mood swing that I can't utter out any words.

"I'll take care of you. You can trust that, baby."

Baby.

I melt against him, desperate for his touch. "I've been bad, Principal Renner."

A growl rumbles from him. "So bad."

He releases me and walks over to his desk chair and sits. Today, he's sexy as ever in a pair of black slacks and crisp white button-up shirt. His tie is knotted neatly at his throat. I want to tug at it and free him from his confines. I want to rip at the buttons on his shirt and seek the hard planes of his chest I've felt before. This time, I'd love to run my tongue across him there.

"Come," he orders and gives his lap a pat.

My eyes are glued to the way his cock bulges in his slacks. A cock I've rubbed up against before and was brought to climax by. One day, I hope to have that very cock inside of me, stretching and owning me.

Slowly, I walk over to him. Our eyes meet and his blaze with need. It encourages me to keep moving forward. When my knees come to rest against his chair between his parted thighs, I let out a heavy, nervous breath.

"Does being a bad girl make you wet?" His voice is deep and husky, authority dripping from his every word.

His palm slides up between my thighs and he caresses my leg just below my panties with his thumb. It makes me squirm. I want him to go higher.

"Answer me," he rumbles.

"Y-Yes."

His brown eyebrow arches and he slides his hand higher under my skirt as though to check to see if I'm lying. When his thumb brushes against my wet panties, his green eyes darken with lust.

"Such a bad girl," he murmurs. "Lift your skirt."

I blink at him in shock at his bold words. I can't

believe we're doing this—whatever this is. Quickly, I grab the hem of my skirt and begin inching it up. He asked me if I was all in. I'm so in, I'll never have any hope of getting back out.

His breath hitches once my panties come into view. The black lacy boy shorts are see-through. Judging by the ravenous look on his face, he can see everything he's looking for.

"I want you across my lap."

A quiver of fear ripples through me and I shoot him a frightened look. His hard glare softens and he smiles at me.

"I won't hurt you too bad, baby. Trust me."

Baby.

I let out a sigh and then fold myself over his lap. I feel like a child draped over him, ready for my spanking. His giant palm rubs my ass over my panties in a reverent way that has me suppressing a moan.

"Here's the thing, Elma," he mutters. "You have to be so fucking quiet. There's a lot at stake here."

I nod emphatically. "I know."

"Can you be quiet?"

"I can."

"How can I be sure?"

I twist and try to look up at him. "I don't know."

He tugs at the knot of his tie and starts undoing

it. "Should we gag you, beautiful girl?"

My skin heats with desire. "Y-Yes."

"Bad girl."

He's gentle when he wraps the tie around the front of my face. He brings the silk band between my lips and then ties it tightly at the back of my head. Drool runs out of my mouth and drips onto the floor.

"I'm going to spank you," he murmurs in a low voice as he opens his desk drawer. Something cool and metal drags along my back thighs. "With this."

I let out a worried whimper and he strokes my hair with his free hand.

"Don't worry, baby. It'll only hurt for a minute. Okay?"

Nodding, I clench my ass in preparation. His dark chuckle has my panties all but soaked. I've never been so turned on in all my life.

"You're mine to kiss," he bites out, his voice hard. "Understood?"

Whap!

I choke on a shriek as fire licks across my ass. Tears spring to my eyes and more drool runs from my mouth. My heart rate is racing inside my chest. I think I might start to cry but then he's massaging away the pain with his palm.

"Bad girls deserve punishment, right?" he asks.

A tear drips from my lids, but I nod. I'm thrilled that he's given up on fighting this thing between us. Seeing him lose control is sexy as hell.

Whap!

Again, he quickly soothes away the sting with his palm. I'm becoming agitated and needy for more of his touch.

Whap!

That hit is the hardest and I can't help the sob that escapes me. He unties the tie around my head and pulls me up to straddle him. Tears streak down my cheeks. I'm equal parts embarrassed and turned on. He tosses the ruler on the table and then cups my face with his hands. I'm tilted down so I can stare into his serious green eyes. I get lost in them. His thumbs swipe away my tears and he presses a soft kiss to my mouth.

"My lips to kiss," he mutters against them. "Right?"

"Y-Yes," I breathe.

He grins. "Good girl."

I relax against him. His cock is hard and straining against his slacks. Without asking permission, I rub against it, seeking pleasure again. He lets out a grunt.

"You think because I called you a good girl you

can come now?" His voice is playful.

I smile at him. "Yes."

"You assume a lot," he chides, but there's no bite to his voice. He clutches the front of my throat with his hand and pulls me closer. "Give me that sexy mouth."

I let out a soft moan as I part my lips. He spears his tongue into my mouth, seeking out my tongue. The moment our tongues connect, sparks between us burst into a raging inferno. My hands rove over him, desperate to touch him everywhere. His hands become my beautiful punishment as he grabs and pinches and slaps whatever bare flesh he can get ahold of. When he pulls my panties to the side, I let out a loud moan.

"Elma," he barks out, his hands stilling. "Quiet."

"Yes, sir."

His cock thumps against me. "Good, good girl."

He holds my panties off to the side and lifts his hips as to chase the sensation of me rubbing against him. I can feel every ridge and vein on his dick as I move.

"Look how fucking messy you're getting my slacks," he growls, his tone possessive and hungry.

I look between us and my arousal is smearing across his black slacks, making it quite evident what he's been up to. It only turns me on more.

"I want you inside of me," I plead. Fingers, tongue, cock.

"Soon," he promises. "Not here. I want you at home, baby."

I melt at his words and continue to use him for my own gratification. When my orgasm nears, I clutch onto his shirt. "Oh, God."

His mouth crashes against mine again. He grips my hip almost painfully as he urges me to move faster. The sensations are overwhelming. I'm spiraling out of control. As stars dance around me, an indication my orgasm is impending, I let go. Closing my eyes, I throw back my head and bite my lip hard to keep a loud moan from escaping. My orgasm thrashes through me until I'm weak and can't move.

"What a beautiful mess you made," he says, his tone filled with pride. "I'm going to make you messy again later when I can clean you up with my tongue."

Our eyes meet and I see so much promise in his gaze.

"I can't wait."

CHAPTER
Ten

Adam

S he's quiet in the passenger seat on the way home. Her cheeks are still rosy from the orgasm she had in my office. I'm dying to give her more. What we had a little while ago was nothing compared to what I have in store. Since I didn't come, my dick has been angry and jumpy ever since. Luckily, when we left my office, school had let out and everyone was gone. I all but dragged her and threw her into my truck.

It isn't until I've pulled up in front of my cabin that I speak.

"Are you okay?" I ask. Spanking her had been thrilling, but I kind of lost my head a bit. All I could think about was punishing her for kissing Zane. I'd been so pissed. It took everything in me not to throttle him. I was about to ram my fist through his nose when I'd seen his satisfied smirk. That little fucker put her up to it. They kissed just to make me lose my mind. And it worked. Jesus, how it worked. It made me realize I was desperate to kiss her myself.

Well, kiss and a whole lot of other things.

"The scars," she murmurs, ignoring my question. "Those are from the war, huh?"

Absently, I scrub my palm against my scarred face. "Yeah."

"My dad saved you?"

I glance over at her. Her brown eyes are soft as she regards me with a sweet expression. I've been guarded around her and it's not fair. Especially since she opened up about her mother.

"He did."

She smiles at my answer, but then her brows knit together as she frowns. "The nightmares?"

I nod. "PTSD."

"I'm sorry," she whispers, tears welling in her pretty eyes.

Reaching over, I grasp her hand and give it a squeeze. "It's fine. Sometimes, when I'm stressed, I'll have more episodes. For the most part, though, I'm okay."

She turns to gaze out the window. "I stress you out?"

I bring our conjoined hands to my lips and kiss her knuckles. "You calm me."

Her head snaps my way and she looks at me in confusion. "I do?"

"You're a distraction. Unfortunately, you distract me from my duties as well." I let out a resigned sigh. I asked her if she was willing to jump all in with me. I'm certainly not backing out now.

"I'm eighteen," she says, irritation in her tone.

"And I'm pushing forty. Thirty-five years old to be exact and old enough to be your dad. Hell, I'm friends with your dad."

Her cheeks blaze red. "But it's not illegal or anything. Who cares if we do what we want?"

Sweet, sexy girl.

"I don't think the school board would be okay with me doing whatever the fuck I wanted with my students," I argue.

She huffs. "Not students. Me. Just one. It's not like you do this with everyone, right?"

"Fuck no. I don't look at students. But you?" I pierce her with a hot stare. "I can't look away."

Her lips quirk up on one side. "So I'm special?"

"Hell yes."

"Nobody has to know," she utters.

My phone rings and I let go of her hand to answer. I nearly choke when I see it's Mateo.

"Hey," I answer, attempting to sound cool and collected, not at all like I have every intention of fucking his daughter.

"Hey, bud. How's my little girl?"

"She's good."

"Good?" He chuckles. "She's anything but good. We both know she's a bad girl. I still have boys showing up at the condo looking for her. If I find out which of those cocksuckers she was sleeping with, I'm going to rip their little balls out through their throat."

I wince and am glad I'm not the unlucky kid who fucked the gorgeous Elma Bonilla. But my thoughts grow dark at the thought of her sleeping around with those assholes. Did they even make her come? Were they careful to use protection? Did they put her at risk?

"I've got to get in and start dinner. Did you need anything?"

"I'd like to talk to my daughter."

"Of course." I reach over to hand her the phone, but she glares at it.

"No," she mouths at me. Anger is written all over

her face.

"Elma," I growl.

She shakes her head at me and bursts from the truck, leaving me alone.

"I think she's still pissed at you for leaving her here," I tell him.

He lets out a heavy sigh. "It was for the best. It makes me crazy knowing she was fucking those boys. Her friend Rita told me she was going wild, making her way through all their guy friends." He growls. "I was fucking horrified to hear that shit, man."

"Her friend sold her out?" My chest aches because that little cunt texts Elma all day as though they're best friends, yet when the opportunity presents itself, she tattles to her best friend's dad.

"You're missing the point. Seven guys, Adam. Rita said my girl had sex with seven guys since this summer." He swallows audibly. "Are you keeping her safe there? Away from any assholes who think they can get in her pants too?"

"Nobody is going to get in her pants," I vow, the growl low in my throat.

"Thank God. You're a good friend. Tell her to call me when she's done being pissed at me."

"Yep."

I climb out of my truck once I've hung up and

saunter up to the cabin. Elma has already gone inside. I find her standing in the kitchen sipping from a water bottle. Her brows are pulled together, a pained look on her face.

"Why didn't you want to talk to him?"

She sets the bottle down and screws on the lid. "Because I'm still mad at him."

"He just doesn't want you to make the same mistakes."

Her nostrils flare. "What mistakes were those?"

"Fucking all your friends," I tell her bluntly.

She gapes at me, tears welling in her eyes. "Excuse me?"

"I know all about them. Apparently Rita told your dad."

The flood of tears pooling on her lids escapes their dam. "She what?"

Stalking over to her, I pull her against my chest. "I'm sorry."

Her body relaxes against mine as she sniffles. "Why would she tell him that?"

"She sounds like a real bitch if you ask me," I say with a grunt. "You should find better friends."

"Like Zane?"

Zane really is a good kid deep down past his hardass exterior. "As long as he doesn't kiss you, then yes. He's all right."

She giggles and looks up at me. I swipe away her tears and press a kiss to her nose.

"You're beautiful," I murmur. "They didn't appreciate how perfect you are. You deserve someone who will."

"Like you?"

"Damn right."

Her palms wrap around the back of my neck and she stands on her toes. "I want you."

I crush my lips to hers and kiss her hard. I want her more than anyfuckingthing right now. Grabbing her up by the ass, I hoist her up and the moment her legs wrap around my waist, I push her against the counter.

"I want you too."

She begins plucking at buttons on my shirt, but I'm too eager to see her naked first. I start tugging at her sweater until it's no longer in my way. Her pink bra makes her tits look fucking delicious, but it too must go. I easily unhook it with one hand and toss it away as well. Her tits are perfect round tanned globes with light brown nipples that just beg to be bitten.

"Fuck, you're perfect," I praise.

Her eyes widen and she smiles at me shyly. It makes me even angrier at the little assholes who got to her first. She's special and sweet. Elma deserves to be worshipped and adored. Those pricks just used her.

"This won't end after this one time," I warn her. "I don't fuck around."

"I don't want it to end after one time."

"Good girl," I mutter. "Once I claim something as mine, I don't let go."

She smiles. "I like the sound of that."

We're playing with fire. I'm her dad's friend. She's my student. And yet, neither of us is stopping. Apparently we both like to play a dangerous game.

Our lips meet again and we kiss hard. Her fingers tug at my hair. My palms grab at her ass. I get tired of all the clothing between us and shove her skirt up to her hips. She lets out a mewl when I reach between us and undo my belt.

"Adam…" Her whine sounds slightly nervous.

Lifting my gaze, I flash her a warm smile. "I'll take care of you. I promise." I won't be like those other fuckers. She's going to enjoy every second of this.

"I trust you," she breathes.

I manage to pull my cock out and then push her panties to the side. My tip slides against her wet cunt, making my knees nearly go weak. I'm desperate to shove into her with one hard thrust, but I need to be careful. With the control of a saint, I fumble for my wallet. I manage to fish out a condom and roll it on my dick all while having a needy, moaning girl rubbing against me. It's a miracle I didn't shoot my load before I even got the damn thing on. With my sheathed cock in my hand, I tease her opening again. I line us up and kiss her. Hard and feral. Claiming.

"Elma," I snarl against her mouth as I thrust hard into her.

A loud, ear-piercing shriek bellows from her the moment I've shoved myself inside her. Holy shit. Fuck, she's so tight. *Too tight.* Her body trembles and a sob escapes her.

No.

Fucking Mateo.

Fucking Rita.

Liars.

"Baby," I coo.

Her fingernails are digging into my shoulders and if I weren't wearing a shirt, she'd most definitely be drawing blood about now.

"Baby, look at me."

Her bloodshot eyes meet mine. My chest cracks open at seeing her tearstained face. Pain has her features twisted up and her bottom lip wobbles.

"You were a virgin." I swallow as I stare at her

pretty face.

She nods. "It hurts."

Another shudder.

"Shhh," I mutter. My lips press softly against hers as I ease her off my cock that's about to explode with my orgasm.

"Don't stop," she cries out. "I can handle it."

I kiss her pink nose. "I know you can. But we're not doing it like this. Not half dressed against the kitchen counter. You deserve better than that, beautiful girl."

She melts at my words. Now that she's no longer tense and upset, I carry her to my bedroom that now smells like her. I set her to her feet and then carefully begin pulling off her skirt and panties. The smear of blood has my heart hurting, but I can't do anything about that now. All I can do is make this better for her going forward.

I yank off the condom and toss it away. "Lie back and let me taste you."

CHAPTER Eleven

Elma

The burn from his intrusion still hurts, but I'm distracted by the hungry way he stares at me. Full of promise. Full of desire. For me. I'm naked and bared to him. I've never been with a man before and my first inclination is to cover my stomach. It's the part of me I hate the most. I'm not skinny like Miss Bowden.

"Move your hands and let me see you," Adam orders, a fierce glint in his gaze.

"I don't like the way I look," I murmur. My shame-filled eyes meet his.

He leans forward and captures my wrists before pinning them to the bed. "Well, that's too bad, baby, because I really fucking love the way you look."

My flesh heats at his words. He dips down and

kisses my lips before trailing sweet kisses along my throat to my breasts. I assume he'll stay there, but he skims his mouth all the way to my stomach. A groan escapes me.

"Adam..."

"Shhh." He nips at my stomach with his teeth. "This is sexy to me. Every single part of you is so damn irresistible. I swear to God my cock has been erect since the moment you stepped out of that car." He runs his tongue around my belly button ring. "I've been hard ever since."

I smile at him. "You're sweet."

He chuckles and bites my stomach hard enough to make me squeal. "Not always, Elma. Sometimes, I'm a prick who wants to bite his beautiful woman."

His.

My heart melts. The moment he releases my wrists, I run my fingers through his hair. I'm addicted to touching him. His kisses trail lower until his mouth is hot above my sex.

"I can't believe this is all mine," he marvels aloud. His reverent words help to lessen my anxiety. He wants me—truly wants me. I can see it in his heated gaze.

His tongue comes out and he slides it up along my slit as though he's licking a drip of melting ice cream from the side of the cone. I jolt up off the bed, a whimper in my throat.

"Lie back, baby, and let me kiss you here."

He's driving me insane with his words. I start to squeeze my thighs together, but he roughly pushes them apart so I'm open and exposed to him. I'm embarrassed, but my need for him overshadows that. He starts a slow assault on my sex. At first, it's just those teasing licks. One after the other. Enough to madden me. Then, he playfully bites at one of my pussy lips. It sends a zing of awareness shooting through me. I'm wet for him and I wonder if he notices. As if on cue, he teases my opening with his knuckle.

"Still sore?" he asks, his eyes lifted to meet mine. With him between my thighs and his chin and lips wet, he's so damn sexy. I can't believe we're doing this.

"I'm okay."

He grins at me—panty-melting and bright. It makes my core clench. Gently, he eases his fingertip inside of me and goes back to licking me. His finger is thick, but it feels good as he moves it in and out of me. My body makes a slurping sound that has me blushing. I'd be horrified except this seems to excite him. His pace quickens and every so often, he brushes against something inside of me that zaps me each time. When he notices my reaction, he seeks out that spot. I'm lost to the way he licks and fingerfucks me so expertly.

I'm happy.

The thought hits me out of nowhere and I want to burst into tears. I've been drifting for months and I finally feel as though someone has grabbed ahold of me before I drowned altogether.

He sucks on my clit and it jerks me from my thoughts. I cry out. My fingers yank at his hair. I need this release like I need air. Adam seems more than happy to give it to me. With fluid motions, he easily brings me to orgasm within seconds. I scream out his name as I ride the waves of pleasure. The moment I come down from my high, he kisses the inside of my thigh.

"You're so damn gorgeous when you come." He smirks at me as he stands. I watch with interest as he flicks off the rest of the buttons and shrugs out of his dress shirt. The wife beater he's wearing hugs his hardened muscles like a second skin. He's beautiful. His body is perfection and it once again reminds me that mine is not. With a quick grip of his shirt behind his neck, he pulls off the wife beater and tosses it at me.

"Hey!" I say with a laugh as I throw it back at him.

He flashes me a megawatt smile. "You were getting too serious over there."

"You just look so…" I trail off as I try to put into words exactly what I'm seeing. Chiseled from stone. Made by God. Like a work of art.

"Sexy?" he quips with a boyish grin.

I bite my lip and nod. "Like so sexy I'm having a hard time believing this is actually happening and that I'm not going to wake up in Coach Long's class with drool on my face."

He snorts as he pushes his slacks and boxers the rest of the way off and steps out of them. "You're here. With me. And stop thinking about Coach Long," he says with a growl. He grips my ankles and drags me to the edge of the bed. "Eyes up here, baby."

I tear my stare from his perfect body that looks even more heavenly and meet his gaze. Green orbs blaze with lust. But not just lust. Behind the burning heat is something almost possessive. As though he wants to take care of me.

"More than a one-time thing?" I ask, my voice soft and unsure.

He caresses my stomach and then gives my breasts a loving squeeze. "I could never have you just once, Elma." His gaze darkens as he reaches for the bedside table. "I'm going to have you over and over again."

I lick my lips when he tears the condom foil with his teeth and sets to rolling it on his long, thick cock with such practiced ease. It terrifies me for a second that I won't be good enough for him. He's probably been with tons of women who were all experienced in the bedroom.

But me?

Despite my best friend spinning hurtful lies about me, I've kept my virginity intact. I hadn't found the right person. But the moment I met Adam, all that changed. I wanted him in such a deep way. It's like everything about him sang to every part of me. I wanted to roll around in his bed and bathe in his scent. I wanted him on me and in me.

His lips find my nipple and he suckles the tender flesh for a moment before trailing kisses up my breastbone and to my neck. His cock is sandwiched between us, rubbing against my clit. I'm still so sensitive from the last orgasm he gave me that I jolt with each of his touches. He chuckles near my ear and then licks me. Chills erupt through me and I let out a whimper.

"Adam..."

"Are you ready, baby?"

"I think so."

He tugs on my earlobe with his teeth before lifting slightly to look down at me. His green eyes are wild with desire and an inkling of pride begins to form inside me. I do this to him. Me. Elma Bonilla. I guess he's not lying when he says he loves my curves. His cock sure as hell isn't lying.

"God, you're so fucking gorgeous," he snarls as though he's irritated. His mouth crashes against mine and I moan. He smells like me, which is strange, but I find it oddly erotic. "Breathe, baby."

I exhale the moment he begins pushing his thickness into me. It burns and I can't exactly say I'm a fan, but I suffer through the pain of it because I want to be connected with him like this. Even if he's the only one who'll enjoy it, it'll still be worth it knowing we're physically together in the most intimate way two people can be.

"Your cunt is so tight," he hisses, his lips hovering over mine. "It's taking everything in me not to blow my load right now."

I giggle against his mouth. "If you come, that means you enjoyed it."

"I want to enjoy it more than two seconds," he rasps out. "See what you fucking do to me?" His body trembles as he kisses me hard. "You make me lose control."

He pulls away to look between us. His one hand rests beside my head, keeping his weight off me while the other one whispers touches all over my chest and throat.

"Look, Elma." He motions with his head to where he slides in and out of me. His cock seems uncomfortable in the condom, but he's drenched with my arousal. It's smeared all over him.

"You're so big," I marvel, my eyes wide. "No wonder it hurts."

He smirks and gives my clit a playful pinch that has me clenching around him. "You sure know the way straight to my ego." He winks. "It won't hurt every time. Your body is just getting used to the invasion."

"I'm on the pill for my periods. If that thing hurts…" I trail off. "I mean, I trust you."

He studies my features for a moment before he pulls out. I watch again as he yanks off the condom as though it's personally wronged him. The next time he pushes inside me, I can feel each vein in his cock. He slides easier in and out and I let out a relieved sigh.

"This is better," he grunts, his ab muscles flexing with each slow thrust. "Much better."

I could stare at his hard body all day long. His tattoos are beautiful. His scars are sad. And his dusting of dark hair in the middle of his chest that matches the trail below his belly button is sexy.

"Touch your tits, Elma. I fucking love your tits and I can't be everywhere all at once." His voice is deep and husky. I'm about to ask what's wrong with his hands when he uses one to lift my leg over his shoulder. With his other hand, he teases my clit.

"Oh!"

"That's right, baby," he coos. "Nice and deep."

I'm supposed to be touching my breasts, but I can't focus. Not when it's like he's trying to split me in half. He's so deep within me I can't think straight. His balls are heavy as they slap against my ass. For a brief, naughty moment, I wonder if it hurts just as bad there.

He pinches my clit again, causing me to cry out. "Where's your head, beautiful?"

I let out a moan and shake my head. "N-Nowhere."

Whap!

I cry out the moment he slaps my clit and clench so hard around him I see stars. I'm going to come again. Soon. No way. I can hardly make myself come on my own and yet Adam walks around like an orgasm vending machine popping them out left and right.

"Don't lie to me," he growls.

"I was…" I moan again. "I was wondering if it hurt there too."

"Where?" His fingers bite into my thigh as he thrusts harder. "Fucking where, Elma?"

"I…"

"Say it."

"My ass."

"Fuck," he snarls, his hips slamming into me out of control. He works some magic on my clit because within seconds, I shudder with a violent orgasm. It sets him off because right on the heels of mine, he comes with a choked groan. His hot seed jets inside of me. It's a sensation unlike anything I've ever experienced. A claiming. Adam Renner has claimed and marked me with his body.

He releases my thigh and falls against me. His hands find my wrists and he pins them to the bed. As his cock softens, the burn from having him inside me becomes more noticeable. It stings when his semen runs out of me. His mouth captures mine in a sweet, owning kiss.

"So perfect," he mutters.

I smile. "I could say the same."

He releases my hand and cradles my face in his palm. "We're just getting started, baby. I have so much I want to do with you." His nose nuzzles against mine. "And to answer your question, it might hurt. But I think we could work up to it one day."

"Did it hurt the other women?" A spike of jealous surges through me.

He peppers kisses all over my mouth. "I don't know. I haven't done that with a woman before."

I run my fingers through his hair. "Seriously?"

He shrugs as he presses a final kiss to my lips before pulling out. "It just seems like something you'd reserve for someone you trust. I've had relationships, sure, but not lengthy ones, and we never got far enough in to get to a trusting point." He heads to the bathroom, giving me a nice view of his toned ass. The muscles flex with each step. I don't miss the slight limp or the nasty scars on the back of his thigh and knee. Once he starts the shower in the bathroom, he returns. His dick is still wet and it makes my pelvis ache for more.

"What are we?" I ask, unable to fight back the silly question.

"We're together." His answer is matter-of-fact. As if it's the simplest one ever.

"What about school and my dad?"

His jaw clenches as he pulls me to my feet. "We'll figure it out. You just have to trust me."

"Like I'll trust my ass to you one day?" I question with a raised brow.

He palms both my ass cheeks with his hands and leans his forehead against mine. "Exactly. We'll work up to it. One day, they'll know and it'll all work out." His brow furrows. "Why would Rita lie to your dad about the guys you've been with?"

My heart sinks. "She always flirted with him. I thought it was harmless, but maybe I was wrong. Rita may have been my best friend, but she wasn't exactly the *best* friend." I want to call her up and ask her why the hell she'd say those things about me. But knowing Rita, she'd lie straight to my face and change the subject.

"The drugs?" he asks. "Your dad told me he caught you with some."

"I didn't do drugs," I tell him, frowning. "Those were Rita's." Always Rita's. "Adam?"

"Yeah?"

I kiss his mouth. "I'm glad I was sent here."

He smiles. "I'm glad too, Elma."

CHAPTER Twelve

Adam

Three weeks later…

"Pick up those feet, Z!" Coach Everett Long bellows, sounding much like a grizzly bear.

Zane waves both middle fingers in the air but runs a little faster.

I smirk before turning to look at Everett. "How's he doing?"

He scratches at his stubbly jaw and shrugs. "He could do better…" He cups his hands and yells. "BUT HE'S A LITTLE GIRL!"

Zane mutters off some curse words, but I see him pick up his pace. He has a slight limp and his face is red, but he's really trying.

"We're getting there," Everett says with an evil grin.

"How's the love life?" I wince because I sound like a pussy. But it's not like I can talk to anyone else about this.

His eyes narrow and he regards me with suspicion. "Fine. Why?"

I run my fingers through my hair and let out a sigh. "I don't know. You just seem happier. I know you're dating someone. Nobody makes your grumpy ass smile and yet I catch you doing it from time to time."

He tilts his head up to the sky and I catch a small smile tugging at his lips. "Like I said," he says, dropping the quick look of happiness. "Fine. Why?"

"I just…" I trail off and pinch the bridge of my nose.

"Is this about you or me?" he demands, a slight edge to his voice.

Our eyes meet and I frown at him. "Me."

His shoulders relax and he does grin this time. "I didn't know you were dating someone. Does Momma Beth know about this?"

I laugh because if my mom knew, she'd already be all up in my business. That's how she is and not just my business. Everyone's. Mom dealt with Everett more often than not when we were in high school together, and instead of calling her Vice Principal Renner, he loved to terrorize her and call her Momma Beth. Eventually it stuck. She had to help him channel all of his aggressions so he'd stop beating up all the assholes at our school. I think he just used lacrosse as a reason to whack people with a stick. If it hadn't been for Mom pushing him into that sport, he would've probably gotten into the bad kind of trouble instead of going to college on a full-ride athletic scholarship.

I glance over at Zane. I definitely see a lot of Everett in Zane, which is exactly why I pushed him to mentor him a bit.

"Momma Beth does not know about this," I say with a smile. "She'd have the wedding all planned out if she did."

"Or the funeral if the girl wasn't good enough for her *precious*." He grins wickedly at me.

"Asshole," I mutter. "She called me that one time. One time. I'll never live that shit down."

He snorts with laughter. "Never, *precious*." His eyes snap up and he bellows again. "Your grandma runs faster than that, Mullins!"

Zane shakes his head but picks his pace up again as he darts around the track.

"She's young," I mutter, suddenly going serious.

Both of Everett's brows lift in surprise. "How young?"

I look around me to make sure no one is listening. "Like very young."

Understanding dawns in his eyes. I expect a brutal verbal lashing from the mean ass coach. Instead, he simply scowls. "Legal?"

"Yeah." I rub at the tension on the back of my neck. "But I could lose my job."

There. It's out there. I, Principal Renner, am fucking a student.

"Shit," he mutters.

"Yeah."

"Is she cool?"

"She's not going to run around blabbing it to anyone if that's what you mean," I say with a frown.

He arches a brow. "You mean like you just did?"

I clench my jaw. "She's cool."

"So if she's of legal age and you both consent, as long as you keep your mouth shut, I don't see what the problem is," he says, a slight bite to his voice. Almost as if...

"Who is this girl you're seeing?" I ask abruptly.

His features become stony and he ignores me to yell at Zane again. "This isn't a petting zoo, turtle! Move!"

"You're not going to tell me."

"Nope."

"Thanks a lot, asshole."

"You see," he says without looking my way. "My girl is cool too. Your girl, my girl, me. We're all cool. You, on the other hand, you're not cool. You're a goodie-goodie hell-bent on ratting your own self out." He turns and pins me with a hard glare. "You're a good principal. I don't want to see you lose your job because you can't be fucking cool for three and a half more months until graduation."

I let out a sigh. He's right. Nobody has to know.

∾

"Everything's great," Elma tells Mateo on the phone, her voice cheery, despite the fact she's naked in my bed. A gasp escapes her when I begin kissing between her breasts. "Oh, nothing. I've been working out for volleyball, so I'm out of breath."

I bite her stomach and she sends me a furious glare. It's cute how she gets all feisty any time I pay too much attention to her soft skin there. To keep from getting a slap to the head, I continue my trek down to her pussy. We've been together going on a month now. At school it's all business—well, aside from the occasional ass whipping in my office—but at home, I can really have her the way I want.

And right now, I want her squirming as she talks to her dad while his friend eats out her pussy. I'm impressed at her ability to carry on a conversation with my tongue lapping at her cunt. I can hear Mateo blabbing away, so he probably doesn't notice her heavy breathing or the occasional stifled moan. At a leisurely pace, I suck on her clit and the lips of her pussy while I fingerfuck her.

At first, Elma was shy, but now that we've had sex at least once a day for weeks, she's getting to be a wild little minx in the sheets. Demanding as fuck. And that makes me hard as fuck. Not a night goes by where I don't sleep with her sexy little body pressed against mine.

She keeps the nightmares away.

With her up against me, the terrors stay in the past.

For the first time in forever, I feel free.

Because of her.

My goddamn beautiful girl.

"I'll see you for your birthday," she says. "And then you can watch me play my game the next day. Love you too, Dad."

She hangs up and sits up on her elbows to glare at me.

"What?" I ask, pulling away long enough to look at her innocently.

"You make things hard."

I laugh at her. "Oh, baby, you make things very hard."

Her lips quirk up on one side. I love her like this, late in the evening when her makeup is gone and her hair is wild. She's beautiful no matter the time of the day, but this time is my favorite. It's a time where she doesn't have volleyball practice and I don't have work. It's just us. Quiet and sweet.

I slip my fingers from within her pussy and grin at her. "Do you trust me?"

She nods without hesitation. "You know I do."

It's the same thing I ask her every time I ease a finger into her ass. Tonight's no different. Her nostrils flare and her focus becomes intense. Gently, I fuck the hole I've slowly been preparing her for. She wants it. I want it. We just weren't ready yet. As I ease another finger into her and draw out a needy moan, I know it's time.

"Baby?"

"Mmmm?"

"I want to fuck your tight little ass."

Her brown eyes darken with lust. "I've been waiting."

My cock is impossibly hard at her coy words. "Get on your knees and show me your sexy ass," I bark roughly, removing my fingers from her tight hole.

She smiles and her big tits jiggle as she sits up to obey my command. I love that she no longer tries to hide her stomach from me. Every inch of her is mine to kiss and adore. I'll be damned if she hides any of it from me. And right now, I want her sweet round ass up in the air.

"On your knees and elbows," I instruct.

"Bossy," she groans as she settles into my requested position.

"You like it," I tell her and swat her ass. My sweet girl loves a good ass whipping. "God, I love this ass."

She giggles and her butt cheeks shake with movement. My cock is practically weeping with the need to be inside her perfect body.

"Tell me what you want," I mutter as I sit up on my knees and slap my dick against her clit.

"Mmmm," she moans. "You. I need you."

"Tell me how you need me," I clarify as I begin rubbing my cock along her slit. She's so responsive to my touch and each time my dick slides past her opening, it gets wetter and wetter with her arousal.

"I need you to take my ass."

I close my eyes for a moment because she can talk dirty right there with me and it turns me the fuck on. "I can't be gentle, baby. I'm going to fuck you so hard you won't be able to sit in class. You might get in trouble with your teachers."

She moans and presses against me. The tip of my cock enters her pussy, but then she pulls back away. Fucking tease.

"You'll probably get sent to the principal's office. I hear he's a badass," I say with a wicked grin. "Likes to bend little Puerto Rican queens over his desk and whip their asses with his metal ruler."

She pushes down over my length again, her wet cunt sucking me in. We both hiss in pleasure.

"He's only got one queen. Me. And I sometimes misbehave just so I can see him again," she purrs. "He always whips me so hard but somehow my panties always get wet."

I growl and slap her ass because she's making me fucking mental with her dirty talk. "I'm going to fuck you so hard, baby. I'll make you cry."

She rocks back and forth, fucking my cock like it's there for her enjoyment. "You always make it better in the end. I trust you."

No longer able to wait, I reach forward and grab a fistful of her dark silky tresses. When I yank her head back, she lets out another moan that speaks straight to my cock. With my free hand, I grab my now drenched cock and tease her puckered asshole with my tip.

"This big fat dick is going in this little tiny hole," I tell her as if I'm narrating our little story.

"I'm scared." I detect a hint that this is true, so I soften my words.

"It's okay, baby, I'll take care of you." I begin pushing into her and I watch her ass cheeks clench. "Relax," I bark. "It'll hurt if you don't relax."

Her body stills and then I see the tension escape from her shoulders.

"Ow," she breathes.

"I know. I'll go slow."

With the patience of a saint, I inch into her as slowly as I can. Her ass grips me nearly to the point of pain. I've never felt anything so fucking good in my entire life. Not her sweet, teenage cunt. Not her sassy mouth when she's sucking me off under my desk. Nothing has ever felt this good ever.

"Fuck," I hiss out, my grip on her hair tightening. A tiny sob escapes her and I freeze. "Talk to me, Elma."

"I—I'm okay," she chokes out.

Releasing her hair, I run my palm down her spine and caress her hip. "Relax, baby. It's just us. I won't hurt you. This will eventually feel good for you when we get the hang of it."

She nods and sniffles. "Does it feel good for you?"

"The best fucking thing I've ever felt in my life."

Her head turns and she offers me a tearstained smile. "I'm okay. I promise. You can move."

I return her smile with an encouraging one of my own as I gently slide in and out of her. Reaching to her front, I curl my hand up and seek out her clit. As soon as my fingers make contact, her ass clenches around my dick.

"Oh!"

"Still okay, beautiful girl?"

"Y-Yes."

In and out, I fuck her tight hole while bringing her closer and closer to the edge of ecstasy. When her breathing hitches and she starts whimpering, I know we're close.

"That's it, baby, come for me."

Her body trembles wildly. It only takes a few more strokes before she's coming with a loud moan. My nuts seize up in response. I slide out of her just as I'm coming. My hot semen splatters against her still gaping hole. It's the single most hottest thing I've ever seen in my entire life. She clenches and everything returns to normal in a flash. Then, she's falling flat against the mattress. Ignoring the mess on her plump sexy-ass rump, I drop my weight against her and bury my nose in her hair that smells like apples.

"Elma…"

"Mmm?"

I love you. I fucking love you.

Before uttering words that feel too soon and might scare her away, I bite my tongue. She's got her entire life ahead of her. I'll be damned if I rush her into feeling tied down in a relationship. If she wants to go off to college and live life a little, she should get to do that. We may have established that we're a couple now, but it doesn't mean her future is decided. Telling her I love her—and fuck how I already do because how could I not—would only pressure her.

"I love everything about you," I whisper. It's close enough to the words I wanted to say.

"I love everything about you, too." Her voice catches and we're on exactly the same page.

CHAPTER
Thirteen

Elma

Two months later…

"It's gonna be huge," Blake Hollis says, an evil grin on his face.

Zane and I look up from our lunches to stare at the wild troublemaker who seems to think he's found his people. Zane and I are not his people. We like to cause trouble in the fun, harmless kind of way. Except for that one time Zane got detention for three straight weeks for changing his grades to straight As. Blake does shit that goes way too far. I'm surprised Adam hasn't expelled him yet.

"What?" Zane asks, his tone bored.

"The assembly this afternoon. Just wait." Blake looks over his shoulder as if to see if anyone is

135

eavesdropping before turning back to us. "Boom!"

I frown and shoot Zane a worried glance. "What do you mean boom? You're not going to blow up the school, are you?"

Blake laughs, loud and obnoxiously. "No, but it's going to be funny as shit!"

Rolling my eyes, I stand to escape this conversation. Zane shoots me a pleading stare to stay with him, but I leave before Blake can annoy me any further. I all but skip to the office to sneak in a quick kiss before the assembly. Mrs. Compton is gone for lunch and Miss Bowden sits primly in her office, tapping away on her computer. I try to slip by undetected, but she gives me a sour look. Ignoring her, I walk past her office and push into Adam's office.

Today, he's a picture of perfection. Strength. Any time I see him, I marvel at how powerful he looks. His chocolate-brown hair is styled and gelled back in a fashionable way, but I still crave to run my fingers through it to mess it up. My favorite look on him is when it's messy when we're in bed. He reaches a hand up and scratches at the dark stubble on his jaw, reminding me that just this morning, he gave me beard-burn on my inner thighs. I bite my lip as I continue to stare at him unnoticed. Since we have an assembly, he's wearing one of his nicer suits. It's a pale gray suit with a powder blue button-up shirt underneath his jacket. He's paired it with a dark gray tie that completes the look. His brows are furrowed as he concentrates on the computer.

"Hey."

Like a hawk, he snaps his attention my way at the sound of my voice. I'll never grow tired of being under his intense glare. All it takes is one look from him like this and my panties are completely wet for him.

"What are you doing here?" he demands, his voice gravelly and sexy as hell.

I bite my lip and bat my lashes at him. "Principal Renner," I purr. "I've been bad. Again."

His nostrils flare and he points at the door. "Close it."

Quickly, I shut the door behind me and turn the lock. "How will you punish me? A spanking?"

He runs his gaze down the front of my outfit. Since I've been playing volleyball and Coach Mink has been literally running my ass off, I've lost some weight and toned up. I'm thrilled about this new development, but Adam pouts when he can no longer bite my stomach as easier as he once could. He's taken to biting my ass now instead. I can't say I'm complaining.

"That outfit is unacceptable." He's gruff and grouchy and all mine.

I look down at my plaid red flannel that I've stylishly tied to show off my slimmed stomach. "What's wrong with it?"

He rises from his chair and I try not to go weak in the knees. I'm absolutely addicted to him. I could be happy just standing near him and smelling his delicious scent. But standing is never an option. If I'm nearby, he always wants me in his arms where he can properly maul me like he loves to.

"Those shorts are too short," he says coolly. "I bet if you bent over, I could see your panties peeking beneath."

I flash him a deviant smile. "Maybe I wore them on purpose. Maybe I like getting into trouble."

He narrows his eyes at me before snagging his ruler off his desk. I brace myself for a spanking, but instead he kneels before me. His hot breath tickles my thighs. The cool metal draws a whine from me the moment it touches my flesh. "Too short. What am I going to do with you, Elma?"

He stares up at me with such love and adoration in his gaze, I'm afraid I'll collapse. My heart aches just staring at him sometimes. This thing between us caught fire quickly and it hasn't shown signs of dying.

If anything, we burn brighter each day.

I love him.

Tears prickle my eyes, but I quickly blink them away. He senses my sudden mood change because he's more in tune with my body than I am.

"What's wrong?"

"Nothing." Everything's right.

He runs his palm down my bare leg to my ankle just above my tennis shoes. I stare at him in confusion as he lifts my foot. When he presses the softest, sweetest kiss on my ankle bone, I beam at him.

"There's my girl. That smile will be the death of me." He releases my foot and rises to his full height. "Anyone ever tell you how goddamn beautiful you are?" he asks, his brows furrowing together. Absently, he toys with my dark hair that's nearly waist long now. Since I've come to learn he loves touching it, I leave it down more and more for him. Sometimes, we're content to just stare at one another while he pets my hair. I live for those moments.

"Adam," I mutter, my voice clogged with emotion. I want to tell him that I do love him, but I worry he won't say the words back. I've dealt with enough heartache losing Mom and then Dad dumping me off. Then, I had to deal with distancing myself from Rita because her telling my dad those lies was the tip of the iceberg of the terrible things she'd done behind my back. I can't deal with Adam looking at me with pity in his eyes if he doesn't harbor the same feelings.

"Yes, baby?"

I grab him through his slacks, desperate to change the direction of this conversation. "I want to suck your cock."

His dick jumps in my grip, but his scowl throws me off. "Elma."

"Please," I beg. "I'll have to go to the assembly soon. I want to sit there with your salty taste still lingering on my tongue."

He groans and his gaze softens. "We're talking about this later."

"The only thing we'll be talking about is your big dick down my throat." I wink at him as I start unbuttoning my shirt.

His jaw clenches, but then he's letting me push him backward to his desk chair. I give him a sassy little push against his chest and he falls into the chair. He never tears his heated gaze from mine. I quickly shed my shirt and toss it on his desk. His stare falls to my breasts that look bouncy and sexy in the new bra he bought for me recently. It's bright orange and makes my skin seem darker.

"Did you eat your lunch?" he demands, his

hands gripping my waist.

I snort and push his hands away. "Yes, I ate. Stop being grouchy. I'm about to give you a blow job. Act excited."

He flashes me a brilliant, boyish grin that sets my soul ablaze. "Oh, I'm excited. You can bet your skinny ass I'm thrilled."

I laugh as I settle between his parted thighs. At his feet like this, looking up at him, I can't help but wonder how I landed someone like him. He's gorgeous and attentive. Everything he does revolves around making me happy. Dad pissed me off when he sent me to live up here, but I never knew I'd fall so hard. Deep down, I thank my father. Of course I'll never tell him that.

Adam watches me with an arched brow of amusement as I fumble with his belt. Eventually, I manage to get his zipper down. His cock fights its way out and once I have his hot, hard shaft in my hand, he lets out a hiss of pleasure.

This.

I love this.

How he can seem so powerful and successful seated in his leather chair one moment but then utterly taken by me the next. It makes me feel pretty powerful too.

With a grin, I lower my head and run my tongue along his tip. Pre-cum beads at the top and I greedily lick it away. His taste is addictive. I can understand how he likes going down on me. There's just something about pleasuring the one you love with your mouth that's simply delicious. Literally.

He lets out a loud groan when I slide my lips past his crown. His strong hands slide into my hair and he roughly collects it all in a makeshift ponytail. I'd offer to pull it up, but I know he enjoys helping. Not to mention, he can guide my movements and show me what he likes. I run my tongue along the underside of his shaft as I take him deep and then gently let my teeth scrape along his sensitive flesh on the way back up. He shoots me a dark, warning glare that has me giggling. When I go back down, he hisses again.

We've talked about deep throating. I've tried a couple of times. Those few times, I ended up gagging and embarrassing myself. But with Zane's help, I've been practicing. Not with his cock of course, but with peeled bananas. He laughs until he has tears as he watches me deep throat the fruit each time, but at least I'm learning. So today, I'm ready to implement my newly developed skills.

"Holy fuck!" Adam practically yells the moment

I relax my throat and begin fully taking him. His grip on my hair is painful as he slightly urges me lower. It's as if he's having a battle with himself. The angel on one shoulder is asking him to let up, whereas the devil on the other shoulder is telling him to shove my head all the way down.

I'm a bad girl so…

"Jesus!" he roars, uncaring of the fact that Miss Bowden is just next door.

I smile around his cock and breathe through my nose as I push further over his length. His cock is officially in my throat. I want to swallow or gag, but I try to silence my mind and focus on keeping my throat relaxed. Drool runs out, but I ignore it as I bob up and down along his shaft. He jerks and jolts beneath me. Every so often, he lurches his hips up as if he's a bull bucking out of the gate. He's out of control and I love it. When he's about to come, I ready myself to take it down my throat.

But Principal Renner has other plans.

He yanks my head back and his cock slides out of my mouth with a loud slurp. With one hand still fisted in my hair, he uses the other to stroke himself to release. I stare at him with hooded eyes as he loses himself to his pleasure. His feral eyes find mine as he comes. Hot cum jets out all over the top of my breasts that are practically spilling out of my orange bra. He drenches me with his seed. A sexy groan escapes him as one last spurt hits the front of my throat. It's warm as it slides down my cleavage.

Lazy green eyes meet mine and he smiles. Despite his relaxed face, I can see the possessiveness in his stare. Mine. His stare is claiming me much like coming all over me did. I'm his. Always.

"Elma," he rasps out. "I love—"

Bang! Bang! Bang!

I jerk to my feet and choke on a shriek of surprise.

"Who is it?" he barks in his authoritative tone that turns me on.

As he shoves his wet, still dripping cock back in his pants, I hurry to clean off his cum with a tissue. Then, I snag my shirt and fly through the buttons.

"It's me, asshole."

Adam and I both freeze.

Dad.

Oh, God.

"We were just talking about you," Adam says in a fake cheerful voice as he starts for the door. He shoots one last glance over his shoulder to make sure I'm put together. I give him a quick nod and drop into the seat across from his desk. It's then I realize

I still have the tissue that's wet with Adam's cum in my fist.

The door opens and Dad stands in the doorway. As soon as he sees me, he brightens and rushes over to me, yanking me up and into his arms. I laugh as he hugs me tight.

"I missed you, angel." He pulls away to look at me. "Have you been crying?"

No, I've been sucking your friend's dick.

"Yes," I lie. "I was just telling Principal Renner how much I missed you. I thought you were getting in tonight."

He beams at me. "I got in early so I could attend your assembly. A little birdie told me they were giving out some awards and you might be getting one."

"It's just for volleyball," I say, downplaying it.

His features grow sad as he regards me. "Your mother would have been so proud."

Now, I really am about to cry. My bottom lip wobbles and I shoot a glance Adam's way. His brows are pinched together and I can tell he wants to be the one to comfort me. Instead, he stands back and allows my dad to do the job.

The bell rings and I pull away from Dad's embrace. "I'll see you after the assembly," I tell him with a smile.

He gives me a quick kiss on the forehead before letting me go.

The moment I burst from Adam's office, I meet the icy stare of Miss Bowden.

She knows.

Ugh, she knows.

CHAPTER
Fourteen

Adam

The show choir dances across the stage and sings their hearts out, but my attention isn't on them. My eyes have parted the crowd to where Elma sits next to Zane. He's got his arm casually slung around her shoulder as if she's his. I'd get irritated if I didn't know better. They're best friends. And truth be told, they both act a whole lot better now that they have each other to lean on. Zane likes to flirt and is a touchy-feely little shit, but he's harmless.

She's mine.

We all know this.

Even Zane.

My girl, like me, apparently couldn't keep her mouth shut either. Coach Long and Zane are the only two people who know I'm fucking the most beautiful woman in this auditorium. When I finally tear my stare from her pouty lips, I find Everett smirking at me. If I didn't have nearly three hundred teenagers staring my way, I'd flip the fucker off. Some kids cause a commotion near the back and I pin them all with a glare that says: knock the shit off or you'll be scraping gum off the bottom of desks for the rest of the school year. They all straighten up quick because I don't fuck around when doling out punishments.

The choir takes their bows the moment the song is over and are about to give the stage up to the band when I hear whispers throughout the crowd. All over, kids are giggling and pointing at the side of the stage near the wall. I follow their stares to Blake Hollis, a kid who spends more time in my office than my goddamn girlfriend.

As soon as I see him pull a lighter from his pocket, I rise from my seat. Everett sees at the same time and is already stalking his way. Blake leans into the trash and lights something. I expect a fire.

Pop! Pop! Pop! Pop!

The rooms spins. I've been hit.

Black. Black. Black.

"Bonilla!"

Pop! Pop! Pop! Pop!

Running, running, running.

I'm going to die.

Right here.

At nineteen fucking years old.

"Renner!"

The popping of the gunfire all around me becomes muted and fades. I'm dying. It's happening. Fuck. I'm not ready, dammit.

"Renner!"

~

Pop! Pop! Pop! Pop!

I've been hit. I'm curled up, desperately trying to protect my organs. I don't want to die. I can't die. I'm too young. I wanted a life—a motherfucking wife. Not this. Not a dirty grave.

Oh, God!

"Adam!"

The scream, familiar and feminine, parts through the terrorizing fog and I blindly reach for it. Her. Soft, sweet, mine. I grab onto her and pull her to me.

Her entire body shudders as she hugs me.

"Shhhh," she whispers through her tears. "I'm here. Everything is okay. Nothing is hurting you.

See?" She lifts and stares down at me. Her face is red from crying and her bottom lip quivers wildly. She's so beautiful.

"I was shot…" But nothing hurts. I'm confused and disoriented. What the fuck happened?

"No," she coos, her legs straddling my waist. "That stupid asshole set off fireworks. I'm so sorry. I didn't know what he was going to do."

I blink away my daze. None of that matters. Not the chaos around me. Not Blake who will get expelled the moment I get up off this floor. Nothing. Just her. I slide my palms to her cheeks and pull her to me. At first, she's stiff, but the moment our lips meet, she kisses me as though she has the power to heal my mind. And I believe her. If anyone can drive the nightmares away, it's her.

"Okay, Romeo," Everett grunts. "That's enough."

Elma kisses me quickly and then stands. It's then I take stock of my surroundings. The auditorium is empty aside from four people. I'm sprawled out on the floor and my head fucking hurts.

"Sheriff McMahon is on his way," Miss Bowden tells me, her voice curt.

I catch Mateo's glare and I swear he's battling between comforting me and knocking my head off my shoulders. It's then it sinks in. I just kissed Elma in front of Miss Bowden, Coach Long, and Elma's father.

Fuck.

"I can explain," I start, but Mateo gives me a sharp shake of his head.

Elma swallows and fights tears.

This is it.

We knew there was a chance people would find out. I just didn't expect it to be this way. In such a humiliating way.

Mateo stalks over to me and offers me his hand. Reluctantly, I take it and allow him to help me to my feet. "How's your head?" he asks, his eyes scrutinizing me. "You hit it pretty hard when you went down."

I rub the back of my head where a knot is forming and wave off his concern. "I'm fine." Our eyes meet and I don't have to tell him. I was there. Back in Afghanistan. Those fireworks reminded me of the gunshots and I lost it.

"Blake?" I ask, my voice coming out in a bite.

"Hawkins has him until the sheriff gets here," Everett tells me.

"Good," I grunt. "Take me to that little shit."

The drive back to the cabin is lonely. For one, Elma isn't in my truck. Every day for nearly three months, we've ridden to and from school together. Now, I'm alone. Mateo wanted to take her home. But I know the truth. He wanted to talk to her without my influence. My chest aches knowing he's probably laying into her as we speak. I'm in a daze as I go inside and change into some sweats and a T-shirt. I've just put my tennis shoes on when I hear gravel crunching.

Anxiety claws at me and I rush to the door to wait for them on the porch. Earlier, nobody mentioned the way Elma and I kissed. I could see the distaste in Miss Bowden's expression, but she didn't rat me out. Coach Long would send me a smirk here and there, but he didn't tattle on me either. And Mateo? He didn't say a word.

Yet.

I know it's coming.

Thankfully, he loves his daughter and is a good enough friend to not embarrass me in front of my colleagues or put my job in jeopardy by ripping me a new asshole for touching his daughter.

As soon as his car comes to a stop, Elma bursts from the car and runs toward me. My chest squeezes in response. Knowing he's going to kick my ass anyway, I let her launch herself into my arms and don't push her away. Her legs wrap around my waist and she sobs against my neck. I hug her hard and kiss her hair.

"Shhh, baby," I murmur. "It's okay."

"It's n-not okay!" she wails, her entire body trembling.

Mateo clomps up the porch steps and shoots me a fiery glare. His jaw clenches and I can tell he's about to go off on me.

"Karelma," he snaps. "Go in the house. Adam and I need to talk."

"No!" she screams at him. "You'll hurt him!"

He winces at her tone but quickly hardens his features. "Don't make me pull you off him and drag you back to the car."

I growl and shoot him a venomous glare that says: fucking try it.

His eyes widen slightly in shock.

"Baby," I murmur. "I've got this. Just go inside."

She shakes her head as she sobs. "No."

"Look at me," I tell her sternly.

She pulls away to stare at me, tears rolling down her face. Fuck, she's so beautiful.

"I love you," I whisper. "So much. I'm not letting anything or anyone come between us."

Her brown eyes seem to brighten and she plants

a sloppy kiss on my mouth. "I love you too."

Once I have her eased to her feet, she lets go. I expect her to go inside, but she stomps over to her dad and shoves him. "You touch him and I swear to God I'll never speak to you again."

His brows crash together and he looks positively wounded. "Sweetheart—"

"What did you expect?" She seethes. "You assume I'm a whore. For the record, I was a virgin."

"Was?" he chokes.

She huffs and puts her hands on her hips. "I'm not a whore. I was sad. I just needed my dad, but my dad needed to get away. I get it. You were drowning in grief. But, Daddy, so was I." A sob escapes her. "You sent me away scared and alone."

"Oh, angel," he says, his voice hoarse with emotion.

"But Adam mended my broken heart. He helped me to learn to love myself, guided me on my future, and urged me to join extracurricular activities. Adam wanted me to make real friends—not friends who tell their best friend's dad she slept with seven people. He just wanted me to be happy. Dad, I wasn't happy until I came here. Now…" She looks over her shoulder and smiles at me. "I'm happy. And in love."

"He took advantage of you," he tries but even

his voice doesn't hold any conviction. Mateo knows me better than anyone. I'd never play with a woman's heart. Especially not my friend's daughter's heart. From day one, she was it for me. I may have fought it at first, but thankfully, love is a force to be reckoned with.

"I love her and would never hurt her," I tell him, my voice harsh and severe. "I'd hurt anyone who tried. Elma is beautiful and smart and so fucking talented. She has the world at her fingertips and I want to show her that world. I want her to be happy."

His shoulders slouch. "I've lost my only daughter."

She shakes her head. "Dad, I'm right here. I was always right here."

He darts his gaze my way. "Don't break her heart."

I stalk over to her and pull her against my chest. Burying my nose into her hair, I mutter the words for her, but he hears them. "I'll never break her heart. She's mine forever."

"Good," he grumbles in resignation. "But if you ever do, I'll take your life just like I saved it long ago."

The threat is heard, but it means nothing to me because I know I'll never break my promise.

I've been waiting a lifetime for this.

$\sim$

"Wake up," a sweet voice purrs.

I try to pull the pillow over my head, but she giggles and yanks it away from me. "Stop, sleepyhead. We're finally alone."

This gets my attention.

I sit up on my elbows and regard the vision straddling my waist. Her shirt is gone and her tits are bare. "Where's your dad?"

"He headed back this morning. It's just us now," she says, a sexy smile on her lips.

I groan when she slides down my thighs and frees my cock from my boxers. It's hard and at attention. Always for her. She peels her panties off and then lines my cock at her already wet opening. Easily, she slides down over my length until she's fully seated.

Lazily, I blink at her perfect, bouncy tits. This position is my favorite because I get to stare at them and watch her neck turn red as she comes. She loves this position because my girl likes to be in charge. Sometimes I let her lead because she looks so fucking hot doing it.

"Good morning, beautiful," I say with a grin, bucking my hips up.

She moans and rakes her nails down my chest. "Morning, handsome."

We grow quiet, our stares locked on each other, as she rides me. Slow and uneven. Unrushed. Imperfect. I desperately massage her clit because I want her screaming my name already. It builds until she finally lets go. Throaty and sexy as hell. I groan and spill my seed into her.

She doesn't slide off me but instead lies against my sweaty chest. I run my fingers through her dark hair and kiss the top of her head.

"I love you." My words are whispered, but she hears. "I want you to stay, Elma. When you graduate, stay. I know you have things you want to do, but I hope…" I trail off. "I hope they include me."

She lifts up and regards me with a watery stare. "Of course the things I want to do include you. Life is too empty without you."

"You're in this for the long haul?" I ask with a grin.

"You're not getting rid of me, Adam. We're going to get married and have lots of babies. You're going to have to build like six cabins to hold all our babies," she teases. "I'll have to have Uncle Zane come over to watch them all so we can sneak in sexy times and make more babies."

I laugh at her playfulness and tug her to me. We kiss slowly and my dick that had softened inside of her is waking back up. "You've got this all planned out, huh?"

"Even down to the carpet of each cabin." She grins against my lips.

"I'm going to marry you tomorrow."

She squeals and slaps at my chest. "Don't tease me." Her eyes grow soft. So sweet and vulnerable. She longs to be loved and adored. Like Mateo loved her mother. I remember their love. It was fiery and passionate and for the long haul. I'll give that to her and so much more.

"Tomorrow. I know a judge. Max owes me some favors," I tell her. "Tomorrow you'll be Mrs. Renner."

Her eyes brighten. "I like the sound of that. Especially because…" She bites on her lip in a nervous way.

"Because what?"

"Because I want to be a teacher. I've come to appreciate your job," she says genuinely.

Pride surges through me. "My mom is going to love you."

Her eyes widen in horror. "She'll hate me."

"Nobody could hate you, beautiful. I love you and my mother trusts my judgment."

"You really want to marry me?"

Laughing, I kiss her nose. "I do and it's happening. Tomorrow."

"My mom said it was that way with her and Dad. They fell fast and they fell hard. He never wavered in his love for her. She worshipped the ground he walked on." Her teary eyes meet mine. "I grew up desperately wanting that love for myself. And I have it."

I roll us over until she's on her back and I'm slowly thrusting inside of her. "Damn right you have it, baby. I'm never letting you go."

Our eyes lock and she nods. She knows my vow is one I won't break. While staring at one another, we make love slowly. I kiss the hell out of her until we both come undone.

"Time to get up and showered," I tell her, nipping at her bottom lip. "You also need to call your dad and get him back here."

"Is that so?" she sasses.

"I've got to go buy my fiancée an engagement ring. And if I plan on marrying you tomorrow, Mateo should be there."

"In that case," she says with a throaty laugh. "Yes, sir."

I wink at her. "What a beautiful start to our

159

marriage. At least you know who the boss is in this house."

She slaps at my chest. "I'm pretty sure you're the one who begs any time I'm on my knees."

Thoughts of the last blow job she gave me are forefront in my mind. Before I can pin her down and fuck her again, my sassy girl climbs out of the bed and runs to the bathroom. I stare after her, thanking the heavens that God didn't take away her juicy ass.

"You coming or what?" she asks over her shoulder, a dark brow lifted in question.

I growl as I launch myself from the bed and prowl my naked ass over to my woman. "We'll both be coming in about three seconds."

Her giggles are music to my ears as I lift her up and fuck her hard against the doorframe, making good on my promise.

Epilogue

Elma

Two summers later…

"What?" I demand, my hands on my hips.

He smirks and sips from his cold bottle of beer. "Just admiring the view."

I turn around and stare at the glistening Lake Newell. It's gorgeous. I never grow tired of living here. The winters are harsh and the summers are sticky hot, but the company's great. Turning back around, I grin at Adam. "Come swim with me."

"Nah, I prefer watching your tits bounce in your red bikini from here."

I don't have to see his eyes from behind his sunglasses to know he winked at me. God, his winks turn me on. Just thinking about them has me rubbing my thighs together in a needy way.

I wade out to my hips and shiver. The water is cold, but it's about the only thing that can keep me cool this summer. It's all Adam's fault too. He always says I'm the naughty one. But he did this to me.

"Turn around and let me see," he hollers, pride hanging on his every word.

Bravely, I turn around and show him my belly. He loves my stomach. Always has. But now, he worships it. The belly button ring has long been traded for silvery stretchmarks. Even I have to admit it's beautiful. As if on cue, our little sweetie rolls in my stomach.

"He's hungry," I tell him. He's always hungry. I'm seven months pregnant with my son and I swear all I do is eat. He'll be a giant like his daddy.

Adam reaches over into the ice chest and holds up a bowl of freshly cut up fruit. "Hungry for this?"

I let out a squeal of excitement and walk out of the lake. He groans when I plop my wet ass in his lap, but I know he doesn't mind. His arm wraps around me and he rubs the side of my belly.

"How's my boy?"

"Perfect."

"Just like his momma."

I pop a grape in my mouth and press a kiss to his lips as I chew. "Just like his poppa."

We spend the rest of the afternoon locked in each other's arms. Adam no longer has nightmares. He says I healed him.

"Why don't you have nightmares anymore?" I ask. I always ask him the same question and he always gives me the same answer. It's our thing.

"Because when I'd have an episode, I'd have to find my happy place. The quiet peaceful lake…" he trails off. Birds chirp in the distance and the wind rustles through the trees.

"And now?" I look up at his handsome face.

"And now, my happy place isn't a fantasy. It's real life. You waltzed into my mind and also my reality. Who needs an escape when they're living it every day?"

I grin at him. "You're such a romantic, Principal Renner."

His lips seek mine and his kiss is full of promise. I may not attend the school he teaches at anymore, but we've had more than one romp since in his office. No one ever ratted us out. Miss Bowden and Coach Long never spoke a word. Dad certainly didn't. Adam kept his job and he kept the girl.

"Is it still romantic if I want to suck watermelon juice off your tits?" he asks, his voice thick with need.

I laugh and pluck a cube of watermelon from the

bowl. "You're asking a pregnant chick if she thinks adding a little food to a sexual encounter is romantic? Hmmm, let me think…"

He doesn't wait for my answer and tugs at the string at my back. "There's my girl."

"Your naughty girl."

"The naughtiest," he agrees.

He tosses my top away and runs the cold watermelon piece over my nipple, causing it to harden. Then, he leans forward and sucks off the juice. "And," he says with a growl that makes my core clench, "the goddamn sweetest too."

The End

K Webster's Taboo World

Cast of Characters

Brandt Smith (Rick's Best Friend)
Kelsey McMahon (Rick's Daughter)
Rick McMahon (Sheriff)
Mandy Halston (Kelsey's Best Friend)

Miles Reynolds (Drew's Best Friend)
Olivia Rowe (Max's Daughter/Sophia's Sister)

Dane Alexander (Max's Best Friend)
Nick Stratton

Judge Maximillian "Max" Rowe (Olivia and Sophia's
Father)
Dorian Dresser

Drew Hamilton (Miles's Best Friend)
Sophia Rowe (Max's Daughter/Olivia's Sister)

Easton McAvoy (Preacher)
Lacy Greenwood (Stephanie's Daughter)

Stephanie Greenwood (Lacy's Mother)
Anthony Blakely (Quinn's Son)
Aiden Blakely (Quinn's Son)

Quinn Blakely (Anthony and Aiden's Father)
Ava Prince (Lacy/Raven/Olivia's friend)

Karelma Bonilla
Adam Renner (Principal)

Coach Everett Long (Adam's friend)

K Webster's Taboo World Reading List

These don't necessarily have to be read in order to enjoy, but if you would like to know the order I wrote them in, it is as follows (with more being added to as I publish):

Bad Bad Bad

Ex-Rated Attraction

Mr. Blakely

Naughty St. Nick
(What Happens During Holidays Anthology)

Malfeasance

Easton (Formerly known as Preach)

Crybaby

Lawn Boys

Renner's Rules

Books by
K WEBSTER

The Breaking the Rules Series:
Broken (Book 1)
Wrong (Book 2)
Scarred (Book 3)
Mistake (Book 4)
Crushed (Book 5 – a novella)

The Vegas Aces Series:
Rock Country (Book 1)
Rock Heart (Book 2)
Rock Bottom (Book 3)

The Becoming Her Series:
Becoming Lady Thomas (Book 1)
Becoming Countess Dumont (Book 2)
Becoming Mrs. Benedict (Book 3)

War & Peace Series:
This is War, Baby (Book 1) - BANNED
(only sold on K Webster's website)

This is Love, Baby (Book 2)
This Isn't Over, Baby (Book 3)
This Isn't You, Baby (Book 4)
This is Me, Baby (Book 5)
This Isn't Fair, Baby (Book 6)
This is the End, Baby (Book 7 – a novella)

Standalone Novels:
Apartment 2B
Love and Law
Moth to a Flame
Erased
The Road Back to Us
Surviving Harley
Give Me Yesterday
Running Free
Dirty Ugly Toy
Zeke's Eden
Sweet Jayne
Untimely You
Mad Sea
Whispers and the Roars
Schooled by a Senior
B-Sides and Rarities
Blue Hill Blood by Elizabeth Gray
Notice
The Wild – BANNED
(only sold on K Webster's website)

The Day She Cried
My Torin

Acknowledgements

Thank you to my husband. You're my rock. Always. I love you.

A huge thank you to my Krazy for K Webster's Books reader group. You all are insanely supportive and I can't thank you enough.

A gigantic thank you to my betas who read this story. Elizabeth Clinton, Ella Stewart, Misty Walker, Amanda Söderlund, and Tammy McGowan. You all helped make this story even better. Your feedback and early reading is important to this entire process and I can't thank you enough.

A giant thank you to Misty Walker for reading this story along the way and encouraging me!

Thank you to Jillian Ruize, Gina Behrends, and Vanessa Renee Place for proofreading this book and being such supportive friends. You ladies rock and I adore you all!

A big thank you to my author friends who have given me your friendship and your support. You have no idea how much that means to me.

Thank you to all of my blogger friends both big and small that go above and beyond to always share my stuff. You all rock! #AllBlogsMatter

Emily A. Lawrence, thank you SO much for editing this book. You're a rock star and I can't thank you enough! Love you!

Thank you Stacey Blake for being amazing as always when formatting my books and in general. I love you! I love you! I love you!

A big thanks to my PR gal, Nicole Blanchard. You are fabulous at what you do and keep me on track!

Lastly but certainly not least of all, thank you to all of the wonderful readers out there who are willing to hear my story and enjoy my characters like I do. It means the world to me!

About the Author

K Webster is the *USA Today* bestselling author of over fifty romance books in many different genres including contemporary romance, historical romance, paranormal romance, dark romance, romantic suspense, taboo romance, and erotic romance. When not spending time with her hilarious and handsome husband and two adorable children, she's active on social media connecting with her readers.

Her other passions besides writing include reading and graphic design. K can always be found in front of her computer chasing her next idea and taking action. She looks forward to the day when she will see one of her titles on the big screen.

Join K Webster's newsletter to receive a couple of updates a month on new releases and exclusive content. To join, all you need to do is go here (www. authorkwebster.com).

Facebook:
www.facebook.com/authorkwebster

Blog:
authorkwebster.wordpress.com

Twitter:
twitter.com/KristiWebster

Email:
kristi@authorkwebster.com

Goodreads:
www.goodreads.com/user/show/10439773-k-webster

Instagram:
instagram.com/kristiwebster

two interconnected stories

BAD
BAD
BAD

two taboo treats

k webster

Bad Bad Bad

Two interconnected stories. Two taboo treats.

Brandt's Cherry Girl

He's old enough to be her father.
She's his best friend's daughter.
Their connection is off the charts.
And so very, very wrong.
This can't happen.
Oh, but it already is…

Sheriff's Bad Girl

He's the law and follows the rules.
She's wild and out of control.
His daughter's best friend is trouble.
And he wants to punish her…
With his teeth.

He'll give up everything for her...
because without her, he is nothing.

EASTON

K WEBSTER

Easton

A man who made countless mistakes.
A woman with a messy past.

He's tasked with helping her find her way.
She's lost in grief and self-doubt.

Together they begin something innocent...
Until it's not.

His freedom is at risk.
Her heart won't survive another break.

All rational thinking says they
should stay away from each other.
But neither are very good
at following the rules.

A deep, dark craving.
An overwhelming need.
A burn much hotter than any hell
they could ever be condemned to.

He'll give up everything for her...
because without her, he is nothing.

He likes her screams.
He likes them an awful lot.

Crybaby

a taboo treat

K WEBSTER

Crybaby

Stubborn.
Mouthy.
Brazen.
Two people with vicious tongues.
A desperate temptation neither can ignore.

An injury has changed her entire life.
She's crippled, hopeless, and angry.
And the only one who can lessen her pain is him.

Being the boss is sometimes a pain in the ass.
He's irritated, impatient, and doesn't play games.
Yet he's the only one willing to fight her…for her.

Daring.
Forbidden.
Out of control.
Someone is going to get hurt.
And, oh, how painfully sweet that will be.

The grass is greener where
he points his hose...

lawn
BOYS

a taboo treat

USA TODAY BESTSELLING AUTHOR
K WEBSTER

Lawn Boys

She's lived her life and it has been a good one.
Marriage. College. A family.
Slowly, though, life moved forward and left her at a
standstill.

Until the lawn boy barges into her world.
Bossy. Big. Sexy as hell.
A virile young male to remind her she's all woman.

Too bad she's twice his age.
Too bad he doesn't care.

She's older and wiser and more mature.
Which means absolutely nothing when he's invading
her space.

a taboo treat

malfeasance

Judge Rowe
never had
a problem with
morality...
until her.

USA TODAY BESTSELLING AUTHOR

K WEBSTER

Malfeasance

Max Rowe always follows the rules.
A successful judge.
A single father.
A leader in the community.
Doing the right thing means everything.

But when he finds himself rescuing an incredibly
young woman,
everything he's worked hard for is quickly forgotten.
The only thing that matters is keeping her safe.
She's gorgeous, intelligent, and the ultimate
temptation.
Doing the wrong thing suddenly feels right.

Their chemistry is intense.
It's a romance no one will approve of, yet one they
can't ignore.
Hot, fast, and explosive.
Someone is going to get burned.

Made in the USA
Lexington, KY
08 March 2018